Beyond E

The story of one of the world's most vicious serial killers

Horatio Van Gelder

kindle direct publishing

Copyright © Horatio Van Gelder (2022)

The right of Horatio Van Gelder to be identified as author of this work has been identified by him in accordance with the UK Copyright, Designs and Patents Act.

All rights reserved. No part of this publication may be reproduced, stored in a retrieval system, or transmitted in any form or by any means, electronic, mechanical, photocopying, recording, or otherwise, without the prior permission of the author.

kindle direct publishing

First published 2022
Kindle Direct Publishing (UK Office)
44 Ashbourne Drive
Coxhoe
DH6 4SW

1

19 months ago

It had only taken Kevin a few minutes to spot his target: the boy was probably about 11 years old, very slim and lanky, and in his tattered ill-fitting shorts and t-shirt looked as if he came from a poor family. *Just the right kind of kid!*, Kevin thought. Kevin liked the appearance of the boy with his dark hair, his Mediterranean looks with olive skin, dark eyes, slim, long and lanky limbs, all knees and elbows typical for a boy this age. He was getting aroused.

The boy suddenly gazed in the direction of Kevin, forcing Kevin to step a few paces back behind the block of garages where he was hiding. But Kevin was certain that the boy had not seem him, as the boy turned around and nonchalantly continued to kick the battered leather football between the few parked cars against the wall of one of the large tower blocks, characteristic of this poor Lisbon neighbourhood. The boy seemed lonely and bored, just what Kevin was looking for.

Kevin gazed around him again to make sure that the area behind the block of garages was suitable for his plan. Scruffy, unkempt and tangled bushes covered the ground which was littered with rubbish

including discarded plastic bags, broken kids' plastic toys – such as a headless barbie doll, a broken plastic digger and a mangled tennis racket – and a rusty shopping trolley lying discarded on its side. An acrid stench of piss was also clearly perceptible, and discarded syringes were lying around, which suggested to Kevin that kids used this area regularly to go to the toilet or when they took drugs out of eyesight from adults. But Kevin did not mind the stink that wafted from the ground. On the contrary, the state of the area behind the garages suggested that adults probably never came here. In addition, and although Kevin could hear the regular drone from a nearby busy dual carriageway, the area was well shielded from the road by a row of dense bushes and shrubs so that nobody could gaze in from the road.

As was often the case during what he called his 'hunting phase', Kevin was proud of himself. He was proud about his meticulous scouting out of suitable areas for his hunt, about his identification of shabby areas full of poor and bored kids, and about his patience not to pounce on his prey to early. Indeed, this was the third day that Kevin had come to this area, always careful to enter his hiding place from the dual carriageway and through the bushes where nobody from the housing estate could see him. And now he had identified his victim. He had spotted the boy on three consecutive days, on the

first day with a group of other children, but on the second the boy had been alone. His assumption that the boy would be there again, again alone, had proven correct.

With a last glance around him to make sure that nobody else was around, Kevin broke cover and walked towards the boy who was crouching down to retrieve his battered ball from underneath one of the parked cars.

"Olá. Você fala inglês?", Kevin asked the boy in broken Portuguese while he approached the boy.

"A little bit ...", the boy replied shyly, gazing up at Kevin with his dark brown eyes.

Kevin took out a twenty-euro banknote. "Would you like to earn some money?", he asked.

The boy shuffled undecidely from one foot to another and gazed around him, but there was nobody to be seen, nobody he could ask or run to for advice. *At this time of day people from this estate are either at work, or probably lying comatose in their flats, too drunk or drugged to look after their kids*, Kevin thought with a smirk on his face. Kevin guessed that the boy had understood him as the boy stared eagerly at the blue-coloured banknote. Judging from his torn shorts and dirty t-shirt, twenty euros was probably a fortune for this boy.

"Yes", the boy answered in a timid voice and reached out for the banknote.

"Not so fast, little man", Kevin replied and withdrew his hand just far enough that the banknote still dangled tantalisingly within the boy's reach. "Come with me", Kevin said as he motioned towards the back of the garages and started to walk away.

For a moment, the boy, Carlitos Viera, stood there, clearly pondering whether he should follow this stranger. Despite the fact that his mum Dolores – and it was only his mum as he did not even know who his father was – was almost continually drunk and unable to look after him properly, she and her family had nonetheless instilled a sense of justice in Carlitos and told him to be wary of strangers. But the lure of the money proved stronger. With a last glance around him and confirmation that none of his friends were nearby from whom he could have sought advice – and would have maybe had to share the money with – Carlitos followed the stanger who had disappeared behind the row of garages. Carlitos knew the area behind the garages well, as this was where the younger kids went for a piss and the older kids for smoking and taking drugs.

Kevin waited for the boy behind the garages. As soon as the boy turned the corner and was out of the sight of the parking lot and the tower blocks of the estate, Kevin grabbed the boy hard by the arm and pulled him further behind the garages. The boy let out a surprised shout and tried to wiggle himself

free of Kevin's grasp, but he was not strong enough to fight a grown man. Kevin turned the boy around so that he could get a firmer grip from behind with one arm around the boy's chest and with his other hand on the boy's mouth so that nobody could hear him shout.

Kevin could feel the boy's bottom against his groin and immediately felt aroused. He felt totally in control now, and safe from prying eyes. While he still held the boy from behind with his right arm around the boy's neck, and with his right hand on the boy's mouth, with his left hand Kevin undid the button on the boy's shorts and pulled them down. Carlitos was now struggling hard, trying to escape. It had now dawned on Carlitos that he was in grave danger and he was afraid, very afraid.

Kevin had now entered a frenzied stage where his lust took over completely. He pulled down the boy's underpants and touched the boy's hairless penis. He had the boy still firmly in his grip with his right arm. He had practiced these movements so often now, it was almost as if Kevin's muscle memory had kicked in, and each part of his body knew exactly what to do to prevent the boy from kicking himself loose.

But Carlitos fought hard. He tried to kick Kevin's feet and shins, and with his elbows he tried to punch Kevin's stomach and groin, but Carlitos was simply to small and light to inflict much

damage. That was one of the reasons why Kevin had chosen a boy like Carlitos. Kevin knew that boys one or two years older would put up much more of a fight. And then there was of course the attraction of a small nubile pre-pubescent boy. This was the victim that Kevin wanted ... needed. Carlitos was exactly the kind of boy that immensely aroused Kevin.

Kevin had opened the zip of his trousers and put his erect penis between the legs of the boy. He stared down at the boy, still rubbing the boy's penis with his left hand, but, as was often the case, the boy's penis was not getting stiff. Kevin knew from his previous rapes that very rarely would he manage to arouse the boys he attacked. The boys were simply too panicked to respond to his stimulation. But he had learned to accept this, to lower his expectations about what he thought the boys were feeling despite their desperate attempts to free themselves. During his first attacks, years ago, he had still hoped that the boys would eventually stop struggling, that they would begin to enjoy his caresses, that they would willingly engage in having sex with him. But Kevin had learned over the years that this was wishful thinking. He just had to think about his own personal experience as a child. But he did not want to go there again with his thoughts. He wanted to enjoy this moment, seek sexual

release, seek revenge for what had happened to him so long ago.

While he still held the boy in a stranglehold with his right arm, Kevin grabbed the olive-oil soaked rag in his left pocket and let oil soak onto his hand and fingers. Again he was proud about how prepared he was, as it had taken him a few attacks over several years to work out the best method to prepare himself. After he was satisfied that his hand was soaked in oil he tried to gently penetrate the boys anus with his left index finger. As was always the case, this made the boy struggle even harder, and Carlitos now shouted as loud as he could for help, but only muffled sounds came out through Kevin's tight stranglehold. Kevin rubbed oil onto his stiff penis, squatted down slightly and inserted his penis into the boy's anus. The boy's anus was very tight and it took Kevin a little while to insert his penis sufficiently to be able to move up and down without slipping out again. Kevin could feel the resistance in the boy's body and a further tightening of the boy's anus, but Kevin was now very aroused and forced himself deeper into the boy's wriggling body. Kevin could feel that the boy was in great pain, resisting him as much as possible, but Kevin did not care. He was now in the stage of his attack where he was just a giant thrusting penis, all subsumed by his lust and the need for release. After only a few thrusts back and forth and feeling

human being in his arms, not just an object to be used and abused. He leaned down and kissed the boy gently on the neck. He saw that the boy had his eyes closed, tears trickling down his cheeks, and he could feel that the boy trembled with fear.

In this more lucid post-coital state, Kevin was sorry for the boy and almost felt as if he should apologise for what he had done. He knew that what he had done was completely wrong, of course he did. But he also knew that he would never be able to fight his urge that overcame him regularly to rape young boys, the urge that indeed occupied all his life and every waking moment. With a sigh Kevin also knew that what came next was inevitable. With a last gentle kiss on the boy's cheek, he snapped the boy's neck with his right arm. Carlito's breaking neck sounded like a dead twig snapping, a sound Kevin had now heard so many times that it had almost become routine. He let the boy's limp and naked body fall down on the piss-soaked ground, amidst the rubbish, discarded toys and syringes. While he zipped up his trousers and tucked in his disshevelled shirt, Kevin gazed briefly at the frail little dead body lying in front of him, but he forced himself not to feel any emotion. He quickly walked away back through the dense bushes towards the road. He peered out of the bushes to see whether anyone else was nearby or walking along the sidewalk of the dual carriageway, and, satisfied that

there was nobody except for cars, buses and lorries whizzing past and paying no attention to him, he stepped onto the sidewalk and made his way towards the nearby airport. His plane was leaving in exactly three hours.

2

The present

Inspector Rachel Sontheimer did not like forensic labs. She hated the antiseptic smells, the sterile neon lighting, the hospital-like white tiles on the walls, the spotlessly-clean floors, and the faint smell of death. She wished one of her other colleagues at Harbourtown Constabulary could have taken her place. But she knew that it was up to her, as the senior policewoman in her team allocated by Superintendent Warrington to investigate this mysterious and unusual case, to find out in person what the forensic team had discovered.

As Rachel made her way through the neon-lit corridors, she recalled the origins of this case. A week ago, walkers on Devonmoor, a moorland area situated at the northern edge of Harbourtown, a city of about 250,000 inhabitants in the south-west of England, had discovered what looked like a human bone sticking out of eroding peat. Rachel had been assigned the case and had taken her colleague Inzuman Patel and a team of police forensic scientists to the spot where the bone had been found. The forensic team had carefully analysed the peaty area where the bone had lain and had discovered

several other bones and a skull, which had been photographed and packed up for analysis in the Harbourtown police forensic lab. As they were at the site on the moor gazing at the few bones which stuck out of the peat, it was immediately evident that the body had been buried there several years ago, and that the site had suffered severely from erosion over the years. This erosion of the peat, which was common for many moorland areas in Britain, was the reason the bones had become exposed and discovered by the walkers in the first place.

Rachel pushed open the swivel doors that led to the forensic lab. Immediately the antiseptic stench hit her and, holding her nose, she had to fight a gagging reflex. Standing around a stainless stell table that displayed the skeletal remains of the body found on the moor stood her forensic colleague Hazel Molfese, one of Hazel's assistants who Rachel did not recognise, and Rachel's colleague Inzuman Patel who shifted uncomfortably from one foot to another while he stared at the human remains in front of him. They all looked up as Rachel entered the lab, and Inzuman waved his hand timidly at Rachel with a faint smile that betrayed that he did not feel comfortable staring at a decaying dead body.

"Hello, Rachel", Hazel stepped forward and shook Rachel's hand. Rachel knew Hazel

reasonably well, although only on a professional level. Rachel knew that Hazel had come to Britain from Italy many years ago and that she was married to a Brit from Harbourtown.

"Many thanks for coming", Hazel said with a smile. "As I told you on the phone, I think that we have some interesting information for you regarding this rather gruesome find", she said while pointing at the bones in front of her.

Rachel stared at the human remains on the stainless stell table. They looked different from when she had last seen them on the moor, when the bones had been covered in peat and soil and were barely recognisable as those of a human. Now the bones had been cleaned which, Rachel realised with a frisson, made them appear much more 'human'. The bones had been arranged in their correct position on the table, and, even as a layperson, Rachel could see that most bones that make up a human skeleton were there. It appeared that only a few were missing, probably taken by animals on the moor when the bones had gradually emerged from the decaying peat. A few pieces of torn clothing were also evident, with one, a leather belt of some kind, lying close to the skull.

"I'll get right to it", Hazel continued. "As you can see", and she pointed at the nearest bones, "we have managed to rescue most of the bones, and we also have a bit of clothing, although most of the

clothing, if the body was not half-naked, seems to have decayed as the body became gradually exposed over the years. With regard to the bones, only a few digits from the left hand are missing and some ribs and vertebrae have disappeared. We are lucky that the walkers found the body now, as I suspect that in a few weeks' time animals would have probably scattered most of the bones, making it much more difficult to reconstruct the skeleton. First you can see that the remains are not of an adult, but of a child …"

As Hazel spoke, Rachel and the others had approached the table and leaned over to better see what Hazel pointed at.

"From the size of the skeleton and dental remains we estimate that the child was between 10 and 13 years old."

"Can you tell whether it was a boy or a girl?", Rachel asked.

"For children that age it is notoriously difficult to establish gender just based on skeletal remains, as bones of pre-pubescent children look very similar", Hazel replied. "But the fact that this body was encased in peat gives us several advantages. As you may know, a body completely buried in a peaty environment can be very well preserved due to the anaerobic conditions that prevail in peat bogs. Anaerobic conditions mean that decaying processes are either completely stopped or substantially

slowed down. Think about bog bodies discovered in many parts of the world that are thousands of years old and that look like they have been dumped there just recently."

Rachel tried to conjure up images of an article she had read a while ago about Scandinavian bog bodies, where the pictures of the recovered bodies indeed looked very life-like, despite the bodies being thousands of years old.

"As we can see, this body was not completely sealed off in anaerobic conditions and decay has clearly set in, removing most of the flesh around the bones ...", Hazel continued.

Rachel was surprised at how dispassionately Hazel talked about the body lying in front of them, and the body of a child on top of that! To Hazel, the bones in front of them appeared to be just forensic evidence, disassociated from the person this body had once been. Rachel glanced sideways at Hazel and marvelled at Hazel's professionalism that allowed her to be completely objective when talking about a body. To Rachel, all she could see was the body of a child, and she tried to imagine what this child might have looked like in real life.

"But there was enough protection from the elements that some fleshy parts have survived", Hazel said, pointing at some fleshy protuberances around some of the bones. Both Inzuman and Rachel flinched, and Rachel held her nose again,

although she probably just imagined smelling the decaying flesh.

"And best of all", Hazel continued, "this has allowed us to perform some DNA analysis. We could clearly identify Y and X chromosomes, which means that this was a boy."

"Can you tell when the body was buried?", Inzuman asked, still evidently struggling with the sad story that unfolded in front of them.

"OK, this is the difficult part", Hazel conceded. "With very ancient bodies, in other words archaeological remains, we can use methods such as C-14 dating which give us reasonably accurate dates, plus-minus a few decades. But with recently buried bodies we can't use this technique. We have some clothes remains and ...", Hazel carefully picked up what looked like the remains of a t-shirt, "we even have a label. This is the only bit of clothing that has survived, and we suspect that this t-shirt might have been buried under the body and was, therefore, better protected."

Hazel held the piece of fragile clothing in her hand for Rachel and Inzuman to better see. Clearly visible were the words 'Harvester', 'XL' and a faint serial number.

"We have taken a high-resolution photo for you", Hazel said while glancing at Rachel, "which will enable you to investigate this further. Who knows, maybe this specific type of t-shirt made by

this company can help us to further establish the date when this boy was buried on the moor. At a guess I would say that this boy was buried between ten and thirty years ago."

Rachel nodded in approval. The label was indeed a vital piece of evidence.

"OK, but what about the reason why this case has been referred to the police?", Rachel asked. "After all, this might have just been a tragic accident on the moor, for example a child getting lost in the dark and freezing to death?"

"Yes, of course", Hazel replied, "but as I told you on the phone, the reason we thought you should be informed immediately about what we have found is this ...", and Hazel leaned further forward towards the top end of the boy's skeleton and pointed at what looked like a leather belt.

Although Rachel had noticed the leather belt earlier, only now did she realise that the position of the belt near the boy's head was no coincidence.

"We have carefully reconstructed on this table the position of the body and the clothes as we found them on the moor", Hazel continued, confirming Rachel's thoughts. "This belt was indeed positioned where it is now, namely around the boy's throat. I am not the expert here on this, but to me it looks pretty clear that this boy was strangled and his body dumped on the moor ..."

Hazel's words seemed to hang in the room for an eternity. *At closer inspection Hazel must be right*, Rachel thought. *The position of the belt, the fact that the belt buckle is still fastened, that the loop appears to be about the size of a child's neck, all this seems to fit the assertion that the boy was strangled and that the murderer did not even try to hide how he or she killed their victim.*

"Again, we have taken photos for you of the body in this position, with the exact position of the t-shirt remains and the belt", Hazel said to Rachel who nodded approvingly. "In addition, I think we can safely say that the boy's body was buried, in other words that a pit must have been dug in the peat", Hazel continued. "An accidental death, therefore, can be further ruled out. We have also taken samples from the peat nearby for further analyses, especially near the body, but, from experience, with a body that old and the fact that the site was not completely sealed off from air and erosive processes, I doubt that we will have anything meaningful in terms of the perpetrator's DNA, for example. But I will keep you informed over the next few weeks as we get further results back".

Rachel nodded to Inzuman who nodded back. They both evidently felt that they had enough information about the body for the moment and that their future course of action was clear. This case had

to be treated as a suspected murder. The key thing would now be to identify who this poor boy was and when and by whom he had been murdered. Rachel and Inzuman thanked Hazel for all the information and left the lab. When they left the lab onto one of Harbourtown's busy streets, Rachel was more than happy to leave the antiseptic stench of the sterile lab behind. She deeply inhaled the air and, for once, did not mind the aftertaste of diesel and petrol fumes.

3

The present

Pascal Lorient was scared. He knew the boys were after him. He knew that he should not have told their teacher that he had seen them smoking behind the school building. He also knew that it was stupid to rat on them, but his innate sense of right, morality and justness had compelled him to tell on his schoolmates. *And now I am paying the price!*, he told himself, biting his fingernails. He stood outside the school entrance, waiting for his mum to pick him up. *Where is she?*, he wondered not for the first time. His mum, an employee at one of the large out-of-town supermarkets was often late, caught up in traffic or held up at work. And she was late again, today when he needed to get away from school as quickly as possible! But he needed to get away not just for his own sake, but also for the sake of the three boys. What Pascal dreaded most was not to be beaten up, but what he might do to the boys in self-defence.

Pascal looked around him. Kids were streaming out of the school, some walking home, some getting inside buses, some being picked up by their parents. There was no sign of the boys who were after him,

at least not yet. But Pascal knew they were coming. There was no way they would let him off after the telling off they had received from the teacher in front of the whole class, with the teacher threatening to tell their parents and the principal if they were ever caught again smoking. The teacher then used the occasion to harangue the kids about the dangers of smoking, especially for 11-year-old children like them. But most of Pascal's schoolmates had just smiled at what the teacher said. After all, most of them smoked or had even started dabbling with drugs, which were readily available in Branlieu, their shabby and poor neighbourhood on the outskirts of Paris. Branlieu, comprised mainly of poor housing estates full of immigrants, had a terrible reputation, even compared with other decrepit suburban neighbourhoods of France's sprawling capital. Branlieu was close to one of Paris' international airports, and the constant loud drone of planes taking off and landing was one of the reasons why it was so cheap to live there. Nobody in their right mind would have chosen Branlieu as a place of residence.

Pascal was a bright kid and could have done much better than attending one of the failing schools in this area. He hated the area and he hated the school. But he knew they had no choice: his father, a drunkard, had lost his job a while ago and the family had to survive on his mum's meagre

earnings. The only option they had was to live in a cheap decrepit flat in one of Branlieu's housing estates. Their estate was not on one of the school bus routes and it was too far to walk home, so Pascal relied on his mother, Nathalie, to pick him up every day. And Nathalie was late again …

Glancing around him anxiously Pascal was very nervous, he was so nervous that he had to pee, although he had been to the toilet not that long ago. Squeezing his penis through his trousers to prevent him from wetting himself he stepped from one foot to another, wishing away the urge to pee. But he was surrounded by the hustle and bustle of kids streaming out of the school gate and there were no nearby bushes where he could relieve himself. *C'mon mum!*, he thought in despair. *Where are you?*

And then he saw them. The three burly boys, the smokers, one of them black, one Arab-looking, and one fat, freckled white kid, had spotted him and walked briskly towards him. Pascal looked around him. He could run down the road, but was unsure whether he could outpace the three boys who would probably catch up with him. Pascal was very small, thin and frail for his age, and instead of 11 he looked more like a 9-year-old. Apparently easy prey for the school bullies! He nonetheless decided to step away from the school entrance, as he did not want other kids to witness what might happen next. *Stupid, really!*, he thought, as he was probably safest among

the throng of kids exiting the school. But his pride forbade him to be humiliated in front of others. And he particularly did not want other kids to witness what he might do to the three boys assailing him. His reputation would be further tarnished, and he did not want his 'secret' to be out in the open. At least not in front of everybody to see.

But he had not much of a reputation to protect at this school anyway. Pascal was a loner, partly out of choice because he found the other kids in his school awful and uninteresting, but also because other kids found him weird. He was outcast by the few other white kids at school for his southern French accent, for not being 'Parisian', and for not originally coming from this neighbourhood, and by the black and Arab kids for being white.

But there was another reason why Pascal felt different from all other kids. Early on in his life, when they still lived in the south of France, Pascal had realised that he was different: over the years he had begun to realise that when he got angry or scared he could concentrate so hard that he could establish a 'mental link' to his opponents with his mind and literally 'suck out' the life of them. As a small child this was only evident when the person opposite him – his parents or a playmate – felt a slight headache and backed away from him. But as he got older he realised that he could increasingly control this mental power and that he could 'see' his

mental link with another's person mind as faint yellowish filaments of energy passing between his opponent's head and his brain. He had realised by then that he was different, even special, and that he had to be careful to divulge to anyone that he possessed this skill – if 'skill' was indeed the right word for something that, he knew, could really hurt other people.

Now, at 11-years-old, he had honed his strange skill to such an extent that he could literally have sucked out his opponent's 'soul' had he wanted to. He had, indeed, become so adept at his soul-sucking 'skill' that he could just apply the right amount of pressure on another person's mind to keep any danger at bay. Over the years, the main recipients of his mysterious skill had been his parents, and especially his drunken father had learned not to beat up Pascal any more, or at least that was what Pascal hoped. As a result, an uncomfortable truce had developed between Pascal and his violent father, and even his mum now knew that she should no longer hit him in anger. But, in return, both his parents saw him as a weirdo, as someone to be avoided at all cost, which made Pascal even lonelier than he already was. Luckily, none of his parents had the courage to speak to others about their son's strange gift. For the moment, Pascal's secret was safe.

Pascal had tried to keep the secret of his gift to himself and had, so far, never fully applied his skills to other kids. As a young child, he had simply acted in self-defence, not really able to control what he was doing. At school, so far, he had only ever had to apply a small amount of mental power when kids harassed him, just enough for them to back off without them realising that it was his 'mental link' that had forced them to back off in the first place. But the situation unfolding now could be very different, as the three boys approaching him fast had sheer hatred in their faces. They wanted to beat him up badly for what he had done. As he ran down the street, Pascal nonetheless wondered whether the fact that he knew about his superior secret power was one of the reasons he had so foolishly ratted on the three boys? *Did I want the confrontation with them to test my skills?*, he wondered while panting and getting more out of breath by the second. He was unsure, and he was still very scared about what was inevitably going to happen as the three boys slowly caught up with him.

Pascal looked behind him. It was futile to keep on running. The three boys were almost upon him. As he had suspected, despite their unfit appearance they were at least as fast as him, particularly as they were much taller than him although they were all the same age.

"Stop running, midget!", the fat white boy shouted towards him, breathing heavily. "We've got you! You can't escape!"

Pascal stopped running, turned around, and stood there, hand on his knees, panting. A calm had come over him, the fear had dissipated, his urge to pee was gone. Pascal did not know why he had been so afraid earlier, he knew that it would be ok. He smiled.

The three boys had by now surrounded him. But they were puzzled. Why did Pascal not look afraid, especially after he had tried to run away from them? Why was he smiling?

"What are you smiling about, white boy?", the Arab kid said with a menacing grin. "I have something that will wipe that silly smile of your face and that will force you never to tell the teacher again that we are smoking in secret!", at which point he pulled out a long knife from his tattered trousers.

But Pascal did not flinch at the sight of the gleaming weapon. Instead he closed his eyes and began to concentrate hard. *Remember the last time dad tried to beat you with his belt!*, he said to himself, allowing his mind to focus. Pascal found it hard to explain even to himself how the 'mind-sucking' worked. It was as if a point in his brain caught fire, as if something inside his head ignited, as if a tiny spot of energy built up and grew inside his forehead. He stared intensely at the Arab boy

and focused all his energy on the boy's head. At first nothing happened and Arab boy continued to approach, his knife raised menacingly. But then a shiny yellowish filament emanated from Pascal's temple and wound its way towards Arab Boy's forehead. Arab Boy slowed down and stood still, gaping astonished at the wriggling filament. He tried to touch it with his finger, but the filament, like a breeze of air, ethereal and massless, dissipated into thousands of tiny sparkles where the finger touched it and reassembled again on the other side of Arab Boy's digit. Arab Boy stared at it in amazement, his mouth wide open.

The filament grew thicker, it was now a yellow radiating stream of light that flickered between Pascal's and Arab Boy's forehead. The other two boys had stopped moving closer towards Pascal and watched the shiny filament with open mouths. Suddenly, Arab Boy put a hand to his forehead and started to moan in agony. He fell on his knees, the knife tumbled out of his hand and landed with a loud clunk on the pavement. Pascal intensified the energy stream with his mind, and now Arab Boy held both hands against his head. A reddish, blood-coloured substance began to be sucked out of Arab Boy's forehead, the boy was evidently in terrible agony. He tried to mutter something, but no sound came out of his mouth. Still holding his head, Arab Boy fell forward, he smashed his face on the

pavement and lay unconscious in a small pool of blood trickling out of his nose.

"What ... what did you do to him?", Black Boy stammered, moving menacingly closer to Pascal.

Pascal just turned his head slowly and glared back at Black Boy, the same intense stare he had just used on Arab Boy. Fear showed in Black Boy's face as he began to realise that Pascal was about to do to him what he had done to Arab Boy. Black Boy stepped back, a look of utter fear on his face.

"I'm out of here!", Black Boy shouted, "this weirdo has killed Ali!", and he ran away back towards the school entrance.

White Boy did not hesitate a second. After a last glance at Ali who lay unconscious on the pavement, White Boy ran as fast as he could back towards the school gate, screaming with fear.

Pascal smiled. Now he knew that would not need to fear these boys again. But, glancing at Ali, he was also worried that he might have overdone it. He touched Ali with his foot. At first, Ali did not move, but then he stirred and opened his eyes. He was bleeding profusely out of his nose and held a bloody hand in front of his eyes in astonishment. Then he stared up at Pascal with an expression of utter terror in his face. He stood up shakily and trembling, and while still staring at Pascal with utter fear he slowly backed up, then turned around and walked back towards the school, holding his head

with his hands and swaying slightly as if still only half conscious.

Pascal picked up Ali's knife and put it in his trousers. He would throw it away later. He knew that he had a much better weapon than this in his own head. But he also knew that life as he knew it was probably over. The three boys would tell others what he had done … and how he had done it. He would be even more of an outcast than before. Maybe the teachers would even put him in an asylum for mentally deranged people? Very uncertain about what would happen next, Pascal slowly walked back towards the school gate, towards his mum's battered Citroen that had just pulled up along the curb.

4

23 years ago

Kevin pulled the thin duvet above his head. He did not want to hear his parents shouting again. He knew what would happen next. He knew that his mum's boyfriend, Keith, was drunk again. Even through the duvet he heard a loud thud. The shouting had stopped. Keith must have hit Kevin's mum, Sheryl, again, probably so hard that she had collapsed and lost consciousness. Kevin started crying. With his mum probably lying unconscious somewhere downstairs he knew that he had nobody to protect him. Nobody to protect him from what was going to inevitably happen next.

Wiping his dripping nose on his pyjama sleeve, Kevin listened out for any sound from downstairs. He hated Keith, he had hated him from the first moment Keith had stepped into their house. Why had Sheryl brought this asshole home with her? *What did she see in him?*, Kevin thought, clenching his tiny fists. *Could mum not be happy just with me and her? Why did she need another man after dad had died suddenly?*

With tears still streaming down his cheeks and clutching his duvet even harder, Kevin recalled for

the umptieth time his father's sudden death about 18 months ago, when a man had arrived from Harbourtown dockyard, where his father had worked, with the news that there had been a terrible accident: his father had been crushed to death by a lose steel beam. It was just a stupid, preventable accident. Kevin remembered Sheryl crying uncontrollably, collapsing to the floor, the gaunt and empty look in her eyes for months afterwards. And also the bills piling up, Sheryl threatening that they would have to move out of their small two-bedroom terraced house close to the dockyards in one of the poorest and shabbiest parts of Harbourtown, that they might even end up on the streets if she did not find a way to make more money.

And then Keith appeared: a bloody drunkard Sheryl had met at the local pub – the *Pig and the Whistle* where all the dockyard scum hung out to get pissed every evening. At first, Sheryl cheered up a bit after meeting Keith, especially as he had offered to pay their rent. She even smiled again and was nicer to Kevin again for the first time in months, but her 'relationship' with Keith quickly turned into a nightmare. Keith was not only drunk most of the time, he was also a domineering bastard, a total asshole who just wanted to fuck Sheryl and who hated Kevin. Kevin and Keith never got on and never developed a close relationship with each

other, the result being that each was trying to get out of the way of the other.

And then 'it' happened! One evening, about a year ago when Kevin was still only 10-years-old, after hours of drinking and Sheryl passing out on the couch, Keith had come up to Kevin's bedroom. Kevin remembered vividly how he had looked up from the book he was reading at the time, an interesting book about communities wiped out by natural catastrophes, and suddenly Keith stood there in front of him, shouting about the 'bloody books' he was reading, and that it was 'time to have a bit of fun'. Kevin had not understood at all what Keith was talking about, indeed it was probably the first time Keith had come into Kevin's bedroom – the bedroom which was Kevin's bastion against the outside world, his own little castle where he could retreat from all the evil outside, from his bloody violent schoolmates, from all that shit that was happening around him, and just sit in bed and read his favourite books about how natural catastrophes affected small communities. His favourites stories were about tsunamis, earthquakes and volcanic eruptions and how people coped, or not, when catastrophes happened. And now this asshole Keith had invaded his space without asking permission.

And then 'it' happened. Keith took off his clothes in front of Kevin, all of them, and lay down next to Kevin. Kevin's first instinct was to run

away, but Keith, although completely drunk, was much stronger and held Kevin back by the arm.

"C'mon, little man! Let's have some fun you and me for a change!", Keith had slurred. "Your fuckin' mum is out of it again, so now I only have you to have some fun with!"

Keith had started pulling off Kevin's pyjama trousers. Kevin struggled as hard as he could. He knew immediately that this was wrong, that Keith should not be there, that Keith should not be naked next to him, that he should not be in his room at all. But Kevin was no match for drunken Keith. Keith violently pulled off Kevin's pyjama top. Kevin was now stark naked, pinned underneath Keith. *This is not right, not right!*, Kevin thought, tears welling up in his eyes. But there was nothing he could do. He shouted Sheryl's name, but he knew that she had probably passed out downstairs and could not hear him. And would she have helped him anyway? Would she not take Keith's side, condone what he was about to do to Kevin just for the sake of Keith paying their rent?

While pinning Kevin to the bed underneath him with one arm, Keith touched Kevin's penis and rubbed it with his other hand. *What is he doing?*, was all Kevin could think of. Then Keith touched his own penis, a shrivelled, hairy, ugly thing Kevin did not want to look at. Keith's penis got big and stiff. Kevin did not understand what was going on.

"C'mon, c'mon!", Keith shouted, rubbing Kevin's penis more violently. But nothing happened. Kevin was much too scared to get aroused. He just wanted to escape.

And then Keith yanked one of his fingers violently into Kevin's anus. The pain made Kevin shriek in agony. Keith went on top of Kevin and with a violent push inserted his stiff penis into Kevin's anus. Kevin cried in agony. He had never experienced so much pain.

"C'mon, relax little boy. You'll be my Sheryl tonight …", Keith moaned as he thrusted in and out of Kevin's anus.

After that, Kevin could not remember anything. He must have passed out from the pain. All Kevin could remember from that first time was that he woke up hours later, his bum hurting like hell and a small pool of blood visible on the bedsheet. He could not remember what Keith had finally done to him. Sherly was by his side, caressing his head gently. Kevin did not understand what was going on at the time and whether Sheryl knew what Keith had done to him.

But as Keith started to visit him more regularly and doing 'it' with him repeatedly, it had dawned on Kevin that Sheryl knew full well what her boyfriend was up to. She seemed to condone what Keith did to him! Kevin did not understand the reason for this, but probably Keith had threatened to

leave her if she did not let him have the occasional 'fun' with her son, and Kevin knew that Keith passed the odd amounts of money to Sheryl apparently 'to help with the bills and the rent'.

Since 'it' started, Kevin had felt utterly miserable. He had already been miserable after the death of his dad, but since Keith did 'it' with him, with his own mother's acquiescence, Kevin had become completely depressed. There was nobody he could turn to, nobody he could confide in. He certainly could not mention anything at school, as even he knew already that this would mean that they would take him away from his mum and put him in a home. As bad as the situation was, he still wanted to be at home with his mum. Even with all the shit that was happening with Keith, there were still the odd moments of happiness with his mum, moments where they would laugh together or just simply do something together like walk in the local park and enjoy counting how many squirrels they saw. Under no circumstances did he want to lose these last threads of normality.

Kevin, therefore, had not told anyone about what was happening. But he continued to be utterly terrorised by what Keith did to him. Although he had by now learned to relax his anus a little bit when Keith penetrated him, and although that had at least stopped the bleeding, it was still very painful when Keith lay on top of him, inside him, moaning and

groaning. It was awful and disgusting, and Kevin felt disgusted at himself. But what could he do? Often, he would go into an almost catatonic state, nothing he could control, it just simply happened, where his body would go all limp when he was lying underneath Keith, and his mind wandered uncontrollably. Sometimes he felt as if his soul left his body while Keith did 'it', as if he watched from a point somewhere below the ceiling the hairy ugly body of Keith lying on top of him and moving up and down, inside him. Kevin learned that this detachedness, this catatonic state, somehow both helped to ease the pain of penetration and also made the whole awful experience more bearable. But there were moments where this catatonic state did not happen, where he was just fully 'with it' all the time, smelling Keith's dreadful alcoholic breath, touching Keith's sweaty body thrusting in and out of him, and feeling every bit of Keith's violent orgasm inside him. At these moments he wished he was dead, that he would never see Keith again.

Still clutching his duvet in despair, these thoughts swirled through Kevin's mind, when the door suddenly opened. Keith stood in the doorframe, drunk as usual, with a lecherous look on his face. With all this thinking about the past, Kevin had not heard Keith come up the stairs.

"There is my little cutie!", Keith slurred, staring at Kevin while pulling down his own trousers and underpants.

Kevin creeped back on his bed as far as he could until the bed board stopped him from moving back further. He wished he could just disappear, vanish into thin air. He held the duvet in front of him, staring anxiously at Keith, hoping that this flimsy barrier would protect him from what was bound to happen next.

"C'mon, what are these shenanigans! You know what's coming!", Keith shouted, moving towards Kevin.

Keith ripped the duvet out of Kevin's hands.

"Look at you, all scared, you little shit!", Keith mumbled with a slurred voice, while he yanked off Kevin's pyjama trousers.

"You know that always turns me on when I have to undress you and you resist me!", Keith said, pointing at his ugly stiff penis. "C'mon, take off your top yourself!"

With trembling hands, Kevin took off his pyjama top. Yet again he was lying stark naked in front of this awful man who was about to rape him for the umptieth time. Kevin wished that his catatonic state – his 'soul floating' state as he had begun to call it – would set in, so that he did not have to witness in person what Keith was, again, about to do to him. But nothing happened. Kevin's

mind stayed inside his body, he was present and alert. Something was different and that was maybe why Kevin's soul had not wandered. As usual, Keith had begun rubbing Kevin's penis. This was an almost automatic thing he did before raping Kevin, and never had it led to any bodily response from Kevin so far. But, for whatever reason, this time was different. As Keith moved his hand up and down around Kevin's foreskin, Kevin suddenly became aroused. Within seconds, his penis got very hard and stiff.

"Well, there we go!", Keith exclaimed with a wide grin on his face. "Maybe there is some life in your willy after all!"

Keith continued to stroke Kevin's penis and the intense feeling increased. Kevin closed his eyes and let the feeling submerge him. He had never felt anything like it before. After what Keith did to him, Kevin had never wanted to touch his own penis. Although the boys at school had begun to talk about masturbating, and Kevin knew all about it from them, he was disgusted at his own penis. But now, with Keith moving his hand up and down Kevin's penis vigorously, it was as if Kevin's whole body had become a penis, as if he *was* his penis. This was a completely new feeling for Kevin and he had to reluctantly admit that he liked it.

Keith penetrated Kevin's anus, but this time Kevin had the impression that Keith did it more

gently. It hurt much less than on previous occasions. Keith started his usual thrusting, slow at first and then with increasing cadence, while rubbing Kevin's stiff penis with his right hand. Although he still hated what Keith did to him, that he was raping him, this smelly awful man, Kevin had to admit that he enjoyed a feeling of intense arousal for the first time in his life. Although Keith's penis inside him still hurt, Kevin liked the feeling of his own stiff penis. Keith increased the cadence of his hand strokes on Kevin's penis, and suddenly everything Kevin felt appeared to be concentrated in his penis. His penis got even stiffer, he felt Keith's thrusts inside him as a pleasant pressure that aroused him further. Kevin felt that he was nearing a point of no return, that something huge and indescribable was happening with his penis, inside his penis, something he had never felt before.

With a loud groan, Kevin came. A small amount of sperm ejaculated onto his tummy, his orgasm seemed endless and to last for an eternity, his penis ejaculating droplets of sperm in rhythmic motion. When the last spasms of his penis had abated, Kevin opened his eyes. He saw the wet stain of sperm on his stomach, he felt his penis quickly growing limp, and he watched Keith above him with eyes closed and moaning loudly as he came inside Kevin. Keith's orgasm also appeared to last forever, but eventually Keith's breathing slowed down, the

tenseness in his body abated and Keith slumped down heavily on top of Kevin's frail and skinny body.

"That was the best one ever! And you came! You came!", Keith whispered into Kevin's ear, kissing him all over his forehead and his face. For the first time, Kevin felt something like warmth and caring from this dreadful man. For the first time, Kevin had not just felt used, but that he had participated in something they both had done together. Maybe things would be different from now on? Maybe Keith would treat him with more respect?

But Kevin immediately knew that this was all wishful thinking, as Keith got up, put on his clothes and stomped out of the room without even glancing back at Kevin.

For a while, Kevin just lay there, trying to make sense of what had just happened. He knew from chatter with his schoolmates and from internet porn sites that he'd just had his first orgasm. But although he should be proud of this, he also knew that the way this had occurred was utterly wrong, forced upon him by this asshole Keith who just used him for his own gratification. He wiped the sperm off his stomach with his pyjama sleeve and also wiped off the sperm that had oozed out of his anus with the same sleeve, and quickly put his pyjama back on.

He lay down under the duvet. His thoughts were confused. On the one hand, he still hated Keith for what he did to him. But on the other, he wanted to have an orgasm again. But not with this asshole Keith! He did not want to be controlled like this ever again. Next time he wanted to be in control!

5

The present

Rachel Sontheimer was always worried when her boss, Superintendent William Warrington, asked her into his office. Warrington's appearance was like many viewers of crime movies would imagine a senior ranked police officer: fat and burly, with a pasty face that did not see much sunshine from a man mainly stuck behind a desk, and a balding head that betrayed Warrington's age close to retirement. To add to the cliché, and despite the many 'no smoking' signs inside Harbourtown Constabulary, Warrington almost always had a lit cigar in his hand which exuded a nauseating acrid smell that annoyed almost everybody who had the misfortune to come too close to him.

Rachel entered Warrington's room without knocking and was immediately enveloped by the cigar stench. Warrington's office was the usual mess, with papers and files strewn seemingly haphazardly across his large desk and also piled up on the floor around him. Some hard-to-identify wilted flowers on the window sill in front of yellowing windows that were never cleaned – *aloes* maybe? – had long given up trying to survive in the

poorly-ventilated room and seemed to stretch out their desiccated tendrils towards Rachel in a vain last bid for rescue.

"Have a seat, Sontheimer", Warrington said, pointing at the only chair in front of his desk. Rachel had long given up being annoyed at the fact that Warrington only ever called her by her surname. Somehow this was common practice in the constabulary anyway, and, with exception of her immediate colleagues like Inzuman Patel, Rachel also called most of her colleagues by their surname.

Rachel did not know what to expect from this meeting. Probably Warrington just wanted to hear the latest about what everybody now referred to as the 'moorboy case', but, scrutinising Warrington's pasty face as he sat down, Rachel also thought there were other issues Warrington wanted to discuss. She knew that she was an excellent inspector, that her hard work and dedication had helped to solve many tricky cases in the Harbourtown area, and that her tenacity and work ethic had allowed her to quickly move up the ranks from constable to sergeant to inspector in a relatively short amount of time. At 38 years of age, she had reached a position in the Harbourtown police force that many older, and male, colleagues envied her for. Indeed, as a woman in a still male-dominated and rather chauvinistic work environment, she felt particularly proud that she had made it to the rank of inspector

by the age of 34, an achievement not many male colleagues around the country could boast with.

"How's the moorboy case going?", Warrington asked predictably and with his usual directness. He was not known as a man for small-talk, but was somewhat also respected for his directness by his subordinates.

Rachel had come prepared for this question and took out her notebook. She and her team had devoted most of the last week to the case and had made some progress. "It is going as expected in a complex case like this", Rachel replied, gazing at her notes. "Inzuman … Sorry, Sergeant Patel is currently going through all reports of missing boys aged nine to thirteen in the Harbourtown area, but, as we have a rather large possible time span of 10-30 years ago, when the murder might have happened, this is not easy. Mrs Molfese, the forensic scientist, has not come back to us with a more refined timeline, although she said yesterday, when I spoke to her on the phone, that they are still trying to narrow down the year of death based on further tests and analyses they are doing. But this could take a while. And, of course, we cannot be sure that the boy came from this area. He might have been brought in from much further afield, which then, of course, means that the number of possible missing boys in question grows exponentially."

Warrington scratched his pasty chin. "What about DNA evidence? Any luck?"

"This is, of course, an important line of investigation", Rachel picked up the thread. "Hazel Molfese has sent off bone samples for DNA analysis but, as far as I know, the results are not back yet. But the problem is that, although we might get clear DNA results for moorboy, we might not find any matches in our DNA databases. After all, our police databases only contain DNA of people convicted of a crime and the chance that one of these proves to be one of the boy's relatives is, to be honest, relatively slim."

Warrington was still scratching his chin. "Hmmm. What about other clues that might help us to identify who the boy was?"

"As mentioned in our report, apart from bone and a bit of flesh not much has survived. But we have some clothing remains, including this t-shirt label", Rachel said while passing a photo of the 'Harvester' t-shirt label to Warrington. "The fact that it came from a t-shirt is itself a bit of a revelation with regard to the age of the body, as t-shirts were only worn in Britain *en-masse* from the late 1970s onwards. At least this allows us to guess that the body is not older than, say, 50 years. Unfortunately the 'Harvester' label itself has not yet yielded any results, as this American company has been around since the 1950s, was very fashionable

in Britain from the 1970s, and still exists today. The label itself, therefore, has not allowed us yet to pin down an exact year when it was made. But we are in touch with representatives from 'Harvester' in Florida, and they promised us that they are looking into it. So, overall, we are making some progress, but it may be a while before we can say when the boy was murdered and who he actually was."

Warrington seemed happy with Rachel's answers, as a faint smile appeared on his face while he nodded towards Rachel. "OK, thanks for the update", he said, while leaning forward and placing his smelly cigar in an ashtray in front of him. "The main reason I wanted to see you is, however, something else."

Here we go!, Rachel thought. *I knew that this impromptu meeting was not just about moorboy.*

"As you may remember from a discussion we had a while ago, I was asked by the Home Secretary a few months ago for names to put forward for staff of the rank of inspector or above to join a UK team of detectives that is to become part of post-Brexit coordination of UK and EU police investigations."

Rachel had been so busy at work, especially now with the new moorboy case, that she had almost forgotten the discussion she'd had with Warrington about this a while ago. She remembered that it was about the possibility for police inspectors like her to join the new *European International*

Police Taskforce, or EIPT, which was linked to *Interpol*, as part of a new set-up to improve international crime-solving collaboration. Post-Brexit, the participation of UK staff in EIPT was seen as particularly important, as rumours had it that UK-EU police collaboration over matters of organised and cross-border crimes had declined sharply. Rachel had been very interested at the time to become part of this exciting new international venture, but had never thought that she would have much of a chance against other, often much more experienced, colleagues from around the country.

"Well, the Home Secretary and her team have finally drawn up a list of those British policemen and women they wish to be part of EIPT, and your name is among them", Warrington said not hiding his pride that one of his staff had been nominated to join this international team of experts. "In fact, if you accept this, you would be one of two British representatives on this team."

Rachel was flabbergasted. Never in her dreams had she envisaged having a chance at this position.

"Wow! That is great news indeed, Superintendent", she replied immediately. "But, if I accept, what about my job here? Could I still continue working as an inspector here at Harbourtown Constabulary?"

"That was the very first question I asked the Home Office when they contacted me yesterday and

here are the details of the offer", Warrington said, while puffing out another disgusting cloud of cigar smoke straight towards Rachel, and pushing a piece of paper towards her.

"The position at the EIPT would be very part-time", Warrington explained. "They estimate that you would spend about 400 hours per year working for them, and the rest you would still be based here, working on your cases as usual. So you could carry on working on the moorboy case, for example. We would just need to find somebody to take over from you when you travel to EIPT meetings in Europe, and, I'm afraid, that is where you would spend most of your 400 EIPT hours a year: at meetings. I can give you a few days to think about it, you do not have to decide immediately."

Rachel had been aware of this from the beginning, when Warrington had first mooted the possibility of her name being put forward for the EIPT position. She knew that working for the EIPT would not mean chasing murderers across borders and doing 'hands-on' detective work. It would be a job that involved mainly talking to colleagues in Europe, and help to better coordinate the response to crimes that occurred across two or more European jurisdictions. But she had no doubt that she would enjoy this new challenge.

"I can decide here and now", Rachel said, with a big smile on her face. "Under the conditions you

mention, I would be very happy to accept a position in the EIPT team. I am sure that colleagues of mine, like Sergeant Inzuman Patel, would be more than willing and able to hold the fort on the few occasions where I have to travel to Europe for meetings. I wish to thank you for putting me forward for this exciting opportunity and even more so for lobbying so hard for a successful outcome."

Warrington smiled back, stood up and reached over the table to shake Rachel's hand. "Well, that's settled then", he said, grabbing Rachel's hand vigorously. "May I say that I am very proud that one of our staff from Harbourtown Constabulary will represent Britain on the EIPT team. It is rare enough that we, as a relatively remote constabulary in the south-west of the UK, can take part in something as big as this. I am very proud of you Inspector Sontheimer …"

Rachel was very touched when she saw that Warrington was on the verge of tears. He was evidently also very moved by all this and seemed more than happy about her decision to accept the position. With a beaming smile on her face she left Warrington's office. It had been a good day after all.

6

20 years ago

Kevin looked around him in the classroom. As usual, he found it hard to concentrate on what the chemistry teacher, Mrs Wilkinson, was saying. Not that he was a bad student. On the contrary, when he put his mind to it he was one of the best in his class, especially when it came to any theme that touched on how human societies coped with disasters. Ever since he could remember, this topic had gripped him. That was why he did particularly well in geography and history, and, more recently, in the new subject of sociology his school had just introduced to kids in year nine. He did not know why he was so obsessed with the theme of societies and disasters. It was certainly not thanks to his mum Sheryl who showed no interest in him whatsoever, and who barely talked to him these days.

Kevin sighed. How he wished his mum would pay more attention to him again, like she had done years ago, before 'it' happened with Keith. But she had never forgiven him for Keith leaving her soon after Keith's last rape, the time when Kevin had experienced his first orgasm. Kevin was still confused about what had happened then. As an 11-

year-old he had not been able to understand the intricacies of Keith's deranged mind. Gazing out of the window, with the drone of Mrs Wilkinson's voice receding into the background, Kevin recalled with a shudder how Keith had come back into Kevin's bedroom a week or so after Kevin had his first orgasm. But on that occasion nothing was the same. Keith was annoyed at Kevin's behaviour from the start, the fact that Kevin had not appeared so scared anymore, the fact that Kevin somewhere deep inside him had almost wanted Keith to stroke his penis, to make him come again. Somehow this had not fitted Keith's warped expectations, as Kevin had suddenly taken more control over what was happening. The result was that Keith did no longer feel 'in charge'. Keith had not managed to get aroused on that occasion, he swore loudly, fiddling with his limp penis, shouted and cursed. After a while Keith had given up trying to penetrate Kevin, got up with a look full of hatred on his face, and had left Kevin's room, banging the door loudly behind him. And that was it. Keith was never seen again, neither by Kevin or by Sheryl.

In hindsight, and as Kevin got older, he was 14 now, it became clear to both him and his hum that Keith had only used Sheryl to be able to abuse Kevin. Of course, that was another factor that had deeply annoyed Sheryl. Instead of being interested in her, Keith had actually been interested in her son.

"He was just a bloody paedophile, using me to get to you!", Sheryl had shouted at the time she had realised that Keith would never come back, placing her head into her hands on the kitchen table and sobbing loudly. But instead of bringing Kevin and Sheryl closer again, the fact that Keith had abandoned her because of something Kevin had, or had not, done, made Sheryl hate her son. With her simple uneducated mind, she just could not admit to herself that what Keith had done to Kevin was wrong, that she had brought a disgusting paedophile into their household, that she had just been used by Keith, and that she had endangered her own son. Instead, Sheryl had turned the argument on its head, blaming Kevin for what had happened, and loathing Kevin for having pushed out Keith.

Kevin felt tears welling up in his eyes. This always happened when he thought about that awful time with Keith, and his mum's stance on this ever since. He glanced around him to see whether any of his schoolmates realised what was happening, but, as he strategically sat in the back row precisely not to be stared at in case he had another one of what his classmates called a 'sobbing episode', nobody looked back at him. His classmates all stared at Mrs Wilkinson who had just set up a chemical experiment involving phials, strangely coloured liquids, and a Bunsen burner, and who had just asked for volunteers to help her.

This estrangement with his mum had meant that the last three years of Kevin's life had been very sad indeed. At school he continued to be seen as a loner who did not fit in, as a weirdo who rather sat in a corner reading another book about how an earthquake or tsunami had wiped out cities and communities, rather than talking to them about girls, drugs or masturbation, or chatting endlessly about the latest stupid social media gossip or video games these idiotic kids played. He hated his schoolmates, and they hated him.

But worst of all was the fact that Kevin had nobody to talk to. And he felt a constant urge to talk. To talk about what had happened with that bastard Keith, to talk about his innermost angsts, to talk about how he felt, about his frequent sadness, his depression. And to talk about sex. Even without being able to talk to anyone about his sex life, Kevin had realised that doing 'it' with Keith had completely messed him up. Of course he had gleaned by overhearing discussions of his male schoolmates how they had experienced their first orgasms, how masturbation was such an important part of everybody's life. From their schoolyard boasts it sounded as if his schoolmates masturbated all the time, gradually learning themselves how their bodies worked and what they liked.

For Kevin, it was totally different. The 'thing' with Keith had made him hate his own body, and

especially hate the fact that he had begun to feel pleasure towards the end while Keith raped him. He hated himself for how his body had betrayed him, how his body and mind had become disconnected while Keith had done 'it' to him. He hated his body for letting himself feel pleasure while his mind had been screaming 'no, no, no, please no!' every time Keith had raped him. As a result, he was torn when Keith had suddenly left. On the one hand, his mind was immensely relieved that this awful stinking, sweating, and disgusting asshole had left, that he would never touch him again. But on the other hand, his body yearned for Keith's touch, for Keith penetrating him, for himself coming like he had done when Keith had been inside him. It was all so very confusing, and even at 14 Kevin could still not fully understand what went on inside his head.

But what had become evident was that Kevin had immense problems when he tried to masturbate. Of course he had tried to make himself come immediately after Keith had left. After all, he had seen how Keith had done it, how he had stroked his penis. He wanted to feel an orgasm again, he yearned for it as it had felt so indescribably nice. But his penis never got stiff when he touched himself. After this whole thing with Keith he just could not make himself come. He felt that he needed somebody else to touch him, or, even better, for him to touch somebody else. He had realised by now that

he needed to be in control over somebody else to be able to feel pleasure. Of course, he had wet dreams, his body made him come at night when he was asleep, but these orgasms were nothing like what he had felt with Keith. He wanted the 'real' thing, he needed it, and he needed it ever more urgently.

Kevin refocused his attention on his schoolmates, while Mrs Wilkinson and a boy and a girl struggled to get the chemical experiment going. Something was evidently wrong with the Bunsen burner. Kevin scanned the boys and girls sitting in front of him. Kevin was still quite small and lanky for his age and he knew that none of his schoolmates would be potential sexual partners for him. He was not interested in girls, another fact that made discussions with his male schoolmates awkward as they, after boasting about their masturbatory exploits, always just wanted to talk about girls, who they were keen on, about which girl they thought were keen on them. Kevin was sexually interested in some of the boys, but most of them were much bigger than him, and Kevin would have found it impossible, and utterly embarrassing, to approach one of them to do 'it' with them. He knew that if it came out that he was gay – and Kevin thought that this is what he was, gay, a faggett! – this would be the end of his time at school as he knew it. And not that he had an easy time at school already. But if it came out that he approached boys in his class for

sex, he knew that he would be totally ostracised, seen as a complete pariah never to be spoken to again. Although, like all other institutions in advanced economies, his school was trying to become more politically correct and LGBTQ-friendly, Harbourtown College was much too conservative for this. To be sure, one or two of the boys in his year attracted him, little Tommy over on the far front right, for example, or Rupert just sitting ahead of him, but, no, Kevin knew that is was not possible to approach them, not now, not ever!

But the 11- or 12-year-old pre-pubescent boys in year seven, the first year of secondary school, were a different matter. In the past few months, Kevin had increasingly drifted away from the year nine patch in the schoolyard towards that of the year seven newcomers at the school. He knew that he had to be careful with this, as he did not want to be spotted spying on young kids. Even for a 14-year-old that would look odd. Instead, he had found a suitable place on the grassy bank, a bit towards where the 11- and 12-year-olds tended to play, but still close enough to the patch used by his own schoolmates so as not to arouse suspicion. He would sit there, seemingly entranced with one of his books, but surreptitiously glancing now-and-then over the rim of his book to spot potential victims. At first, it had felt rather weird and he had not at all been comfortable with his own behaviour, or sure

whether this was the right thing to do at this point in time.

But then he saw him. A young-looking blond and thin 11- or 12-year-old boy with shoulder long hair, a dreamy look on his angelic face, standing a bit lost and apart from his schoolmates. To Kevin's eyes, the boy was beautiful, all knees and elbows in his poorly fitting school shorts and badly-tucked-in shirt, with a shy smile on his face, lost in thought. Kevin knew that, if need be, even himself with his small stature could overpower that small boy, could exert control over him, could force the boy to do things, maybe even to do 'it' with him. While watching the boy Kevin had become aroused and had glanced around him to see whether anyone had spotted the embarrassing bulge in his trousers. But nobody cared about him, not his classmates who had long given up trying to interact with him, nor the 11- and 12-year-olds who were all engrossed in their still rather childish schoolyard games, the girls clustering in groups and talking, the boys kicking footballs or checking out each other's latest gimmicks on their mobile phones. Only the little blond boy stood apart, somehow lost in his own small inscrutable world.

Kevin remembered staring at the blond boy for a long time, but lowering his gaze towards his book regularly so as not to be spotted staring at the boy. Kevin did not know the boy's name, nor was he

very interested what the boy was called. To Kevin, this boy had become an instrument of his distorted sexual fantasy, a focal point for his warped sexual mind, a target that made his days, and nights, more liveable for the first time in many years. Every day, Kevin came back to the same spot on the grassy bank, hoping to catch a glimpse of blond boy. When he saw the boy, Kevin always felt a warm feeling in his body, but especially in his loins. For the first time, he was happy.

Glancing out of the window, with the distant drone of Mrs Wilkinson's cheers in the background as she had finally managed to get her stupid experiment going, Kevin smiled. He knew that he had a plan now, that he had something to look forward to, that he found a possible solution to vent his sexual frustration. Very soon, he would set his plan into motion. He just needed to find the right occasion.

7

The present

Pascal sat on his hands and moved nervously from one side to the other, his feet tapping the wooden floor of the principal's office with a loud staccato. Nathalie, sitting next to Pascal, and with an anxious look on her face, put a hand on Pascal's knee to stop the tapping noise. Pascal did not know whether his mum would take his side in this whole unfortunate affair. She had been so weird to him lately, so unmotherly, so remote, as if an invisible barrier had appeared between them.

"Alors Pascal Lorient, what shall we do with you?", the principal, sitting behind a large wooden desk and towering over tiny Pascal, asked, taking Pascal out of his thoughts. "I am worried about you", the principal continued. "You should know that we can't condone such behaviour at our lycée!"

"I was just defending myself!", Pascal retorted forcefully. Nathalie squeezed his knee more tightly and looked at him with a stare that unquestioningly told Pascal to be less bolshy.

"Sorry, monsieur le principal", Pascal said with a more emollient tone, "but these boys attacked me and I had to defend myself." But he did not want to

tell the principal that a knife had been involved as he had thrown away Arab boy's knife after the attack and, therefore, had no evidence to back up this side of the story.

"That may well be the case, but ...", and the principal ruffled through some papers on the desk in front of him, "... Ali Ibn Caid was severely injured during your fight. He had to go to hospital and was diagnosed with bleeding on the brain. That is a severe injury as I am sure you will know ..." The principal looked down at Pascal, and it was evident that he found it hard to believe that such a fragile-looking small and thin boy could defeat three burly bullies much taller than him. Something in this story did not add up.

"I know nothing about this, monsieur le principal", Pascal replied timidly. "All I know is that they attacked me and that Ali must have slipped ... or something ... and hit bis head. Then they all fled ..."

Pascal felt Nathalie stare back at him. He knew that she fully understood what had happened to Ali. After all, Nathalie had witnessed herself what Pascal could do, both to herself when she got angry with her son, and especially to Pascal's father, Simon, who had ended up lying unconscious in his own vomit after his last attempt to beat up Pascal in one of his drunken violent outbursts. Pascal glanced at his mum and could see a mixture of

incomprehension and fear in her haggard and prematurely wrinkled face. Although Pascal knew that he would not get much sympathy from Nathalie with regard to this latest incident, he at least hoped that she would keep quiet about what she knew about Pascal's special 'gift'.

"I have the word of the three boys against yours, Pascal", the principal said in a tone that did not invite any riposte, and while playing nervously with a pencil in his left hand. The principal paused and was lost in thought for a moment. "But I am willing to believe on this occasion that what happened to Ali might have just been an accident. After all, it is hard to imagine that a … a frail boy like you …", the principal continued, looking apologetically towards Nathalie, " … yes, a frail boy like you could inflict real harm on these three … these three bullies who are known for their cruelty towards other school children."

Could Pascal even detect a sense that the principal was somehow proud of how Pascal had been able to stand up to his three attackers? A faint smile on the principal's face and a conspiratorial glance between the principal and Pascal seemed to confirm Pascal's hunch.

"So we will let this matter rest, at least for the moment, and luckily no charges have been pressed by Ali Ibn Caid's parents", the principal continued, regaining his school-masterly poise. "But this is a

warning to you, monsieur Lorient: one more report like this that involves you harming another schoolmate and this will have severe consequences. Do you understand what I am saying?"

Pascal nodded. He was pleased with what he heard, and he could also feel Nathalie's hand relax on his knee. It seemed that he had got away with what he had done to Ali. But he knew that he had to be even more careful than before. He could not risk being locked away because of his gift. Even considering his problematic situation at home, Pascal knew that he would not cope with being taken into care or, even worse, being incarcerated in a children's psychiatric hospital because of his 'special gift'.

Nathalie motioned to Pascal to get up and they both thanked the principal for his time and candour. But as they left the principal's office, Pascal could not prevent himself seeing the worried look on his mother's face. Indeed, she seemed absolutely terrified and did not dare look back into her son's face as they slowly walked down the corridor.

8

16 months ago

Kevin gazed out of the window in the small seminar room. He was bored and he could not wait for the workshop to finish. He glanced at his watch. Another 15 minutes until the official end of the workshop! He knew that there would be drinks and canapés afterwards, as academics just loved chatting and drinking. Often Kevin had the impression that the workshops and conferences he regularly attended were more about eating, chatting and drinking then about research. But he did not care anyway. His purpose for being here was not research and meeting like-minded colleagues who worked on themes of community resilience. It was just sheer, depraved lust.

It had been three months since Kevin's trip to Portugal, and in his mind he had over-and-over replayed the pleasure he had felt when he had raped the Portuguese boy in the estate near Lisbon airport. Like a film, he repeatedly replayed every scene of the rape in his mind, how he had cunningly lured the boy behind the garages, how he had yanked off the boy's trousers and fondled the boy's penis, the lust he had felt when he had penetrated the boy and had

come inside him. Even the frustration of not being able to arouse the boy was overshadowed by the pleasant memory of the sexual pleasure he felt when taking the boy from behind. The part of the scene that Kevin blanked out was the actual murder of his victim. For him, that was just sheer necessity and not part of the act. It just had to be done, but it was not why he attacked these boys. The control he exerted came not from the killing, it came from the sexual domination of his victims. But he could not let them live. This was simply too dangerous. They would inform on him and identify him. He could never let that happen.

But ever since he had started attacking and raping young boys, the problem was that his memories of the acts both faded after a few months and became increasingly intertwined, making it more difficult to remember very specific details. He had thought about filming what he did with his mobile phone and had even shot a short film showing his penis moving in and out of the anus of a boy he had raped in Brussels. But even though the filming had been successful in the dim light, and although he had managed to just about hold on to his young victim with just one arm while filming, when he had approached airport security on the way back panic had overtaken him. Images of security staff checking the contents of his phone and uncovering his whole unsavoury deeds sprang up in

his mind and he panicked. The result was that he had deleted the clip on his phone there and then, swearing that he would never film himself in the act again. Nor would he ever keep a memento of the boys he had raped – their underpants, a lock from their hair, a t-shirt with their sweet smell impregnated in it. There should never be any proof of what he did! The pictures should be etched in his mind and nowhere else! But the downside was that his mind started to forget, the clarity of the images in his head began to fade with time, scenes of rape of different boys blurred into one another, the pleasure he felt conjuring up the images of his rapes receded more quickly, meaning that he had to find another boy again soon.

And he still could not relieve himself sexually through masturbation. Ever since the episode as a young boy with awful Keith, his body refused to be aroused by his own stimulation. He only got aroused when he saw young boys, and he could only reach a climax when he actually raped boys. Wet dreams continued to haunt him at night, even now as an adult, but he took no pleasure in them. This meant that on top of memories of his last depraved rapes fading, with every passing month his sexual pressure increased, the need for release intensified, the urge to rape again grew. And for strategic reasons, the rapes had to take place outside the UK, in different European countries where it would be

much harder to trace him, to match his DNA, to connect the dots of his depraved trail together.

Kevin had been lucky. Only three weeks earlier had he been told by a colleague about a forthcoming workshop on 'The resilience of small mountain communities in the European Alps', hosted by sociologists at the University of Geneva. The European colleagues were more than happy to offer him a place in the workshop – in most cases these events were under-subscribed due to the fact that most European academics lacked generous grants that covered flight and accommodation expenses – and he still had plenty of money left in his research account that would easily cover the expenses of the trip. Kevin had managed to book the last seat on an EasyJet flight from Bristol to Geneva, and now he sat there, twiddling his thumbs and bored to death while he listened to the closing comments of their dull female academic host.

The workshop had lasted three days, but after playing the game and dutifully listening to rather boring papers delivered by his European colleagues on the first day, Kevin had used the second day to explore one of the less salubrious neighbourhoods of Geneva. This was the first time he had chosen a Swiss destination for his plans, and he was well aware that he had to be particularly careful in a country with a strong reputation for assiduously following the rule of law and, worse of all, dotted

with street cameras in many urban areas. Kevin's first task had, therefore, been to scout out deprived areas where he could be sure that no video footage of him would be available. After scrutinising his town plan and walking for a few hours through various neighbourhoods, feigning to be a lost tourist, he had discovered the suburb of Clemenceau not too far from the airport.

No part of Geneva was really poor, that just simply did not exist in wealthy Switzerland, but Kevin was nonetheless surprised to see the level of deprivation evident in Clemenceau. As was often the case with poorer neighbourhoods in European cities, this suburb was full of immigrants and hardly a white face could be seen. Kevin had underestimated how many non-Swiss citizens actually lived in Switzerland and had been surprised to learn that almost two thirds of people in the canton of Geneva were of non-Swiss origin. As Kevin walked through the back streets of Clemenceau, Kevin looked out for children. School finished early in Switzerland, and at three o'clock on a sunny afternoon, the streets and parks bustled with kids and families.

Kevin was on the lookout for two things. First and foremost was a suitable location, similar to the one he had found in Lisbon three months earlier: poor, secluded, and with semi-derelict buildings or garages where he could perform the rape. He

preferred housing estates built in the mid to late 20th century, as these often comprised harder-to-monitor cul-de-sac locations preferred by planners of that era. Second, he had to find a boy of the right age, slim and fragile so that he could easily overpower and control him and, most importantly, a boy who Kevin would find attractive and who would sexually arouse him. On the latter issue, Kevin did not mind whether the boy was white, black or Asian, with blond, brown or black hair. His 'taste' for boys was relatively eclectic as long as the boys were slim and slender with nice faces and thin limbs.

Invoking images of boys he had selected over the past few years aroused Kevin. He quickened his pace and approached what looked like a big housing estate comprised of five- to seven-story apartment blocks that looked grimy, dirty and poorly maintained in a very un-Swiss-like fashion. Kevin always tried to find such housing estates which, he thought, all looked pretty much the same around Europe: the same poor planning, the same dreadful facades, the same overemphasis on cars and parking, and rubbish everywhere. These were places nobody cared about, unloved places without pride or a real sense of ownership, forgotten places where parents were also less likely to look after their kids. Indeed, parents were often so preoccupied with their own sorry lives that their

kids often were let loose to do what they wanted. Only when their kids did not turn up for dinner would these parents begin to worry. But by this time it was too late: by the time the body of their son was discovered, Kevin's deed would have long been done, he would be on a plane back, or even already in the UK. This was the advantage of committing the rape just a few hours before Kevin's flight back. By the time the police would discover the body – and even Kevin's sperm inside his victim's body – Kevin would be back home, in a different jurisdiction, and now, since Brexit, even outside the EU. How could they ever catch him?

Kevin had found what he was looking for in the suburb of Clemenceau: a dishevelled housing estate probably built in the 1970s or 1980s, plenty of kids running around unattended, and a row of garages behind which it would be easy to hide. Kevin made his way to the back of one of the rows of garages and was satisfied to see that nobody seemed to be watching him. From here he had a good view towards a rubbish-strewn playground – again very un-Swiss like, Kevin thought – and several kids of all ages playing, cycling, or kicking footballs around. One boy, possibly of Pakistani origin particularly caught his attention.

But Kevin did not want to linger for fear of being detected. He knew he had found a good place, he would come back here just after the workshop

and before his return flight left for Bristol. As he walked back towards his accommodation at the university he was happy. Finally he would be able to satisfy his sexual appetite again. Three months had been too long a time for abstinence.

9

The present

Rachel was still half asleep as her left hand tried to feel him. But there was nobody lying next to her in bed. She opened her eyes and stared at the crumpled bedsheets on the other side of her bed. He was gone again! *And not the first time this has happened!*, she thought furiously. She propped herself up against the headboard, naked and not bothering to cover herself with a blanket. And she had so hoped that they would make love again first thing after waking up. How she wished he would be there, so that she could cuddle up against him, feel his warmth.

Stupid! I'm so stupid!, she berated herself, pounding the sides of her head with her fists. *Why can't I just break up with Gordon! I know he will always run back to his wife after we've made love. It happens all the time! I think that this time he will stay with me all night, make love again in the morning, but no ... as soon as I'm asleep he flees, disappears, absconds ... He is just using me, using me!*, she almost said the last part of her thoughts aloud, pounding her head harder. *I should've never let myself in with a married bloke! What a mistake!*

But it had not been the first time that she had fallen for a married guy. Indeed, it was the third time this had happened in a row. And she somehow loved Gordon, or at least she thought she did. She certainly liked the love-making, and Gordon was very good at it. He knew exactly how to read what she wanted and when she wanted it, and he certainly did the best oral sex she had ever experienced, even better than her former, also married, lover Grant. As she put on her clothes, discarded next to the bed in a tangled heap the evening before when Gordon and her had jumped into bed, she berated herself over and over in her choice of men. "Why can't you just find a nice unmarried bloke, get married, have kids?", she said to herself aloud, her voice sounding strangely echoey and hollow in the hallway on the way to the kitchen.

She switched on the coffee machine, took two frozen slices of toast out of the freezer and popped them into the toaster. As she prepared a plate and cutlery her thoughts turned, yet again, to her age. At 38, Rachel knew that it was almost too late to find a stable partner and have kids. Her biological clock was ticking, and she hated it! She still was unsure whether she wanted kids, with her job and her otherwise busy life, but her girlfriends who eventually had kids had all said that you somehow always find the time for the kids once you have them, as everything else is pushed aside, especially

in the first few years. But did she want everything to be pushed aside, especially her job which she really enjoyed? She gazed pensively out of the window. What did she want? Was she happy with her current life?

The new opportunities in her job certainly made her happy. Her selection as one of two British representatives on the *European International Police Taskforce* was incredibly exciting, she could not wait to start. How would having a kid fit into this long-term European commitment which would often take her abroad? Rachel suddenly had visions of her standing in the porch with her suitcase packed but unable to go to the next EIPT meeting because she had not been able to arrange a babysitter. And even if she still wanted a kid, how would she find the right partner? All these married men she had been with over the past few years had somehow drifted towards her. It was not so much her doing, it was more luck, or bad luck, in that these men were at the right place at the right time and, she had to admit, every time she met one of them she had been horny. She needed regular sex with men, she wanted men. And these married men – Gordon, Grant and the others – had been there, available, usually at parties or at gatherings with friends.

With a wry smile and while munching her toast, Rachel remembered the first love-making with Gordon. She had been invited to her friend Naomi

for a small party, 'just some friends and their partners' Naomi had lured her to come, and there he was: Gordon, good-looking, about her age, with a glass of whisky in his hand and staring at her from the moment she had arrived at Naomi's place. Even today, Rachel was unsure whether Gordon's wife had also been at Naomi's party, and if she was she must have been very busy herself indeed! It only took Rachel and Gordon a few minutes before they absconded into the first vacant bedroom, possibly even Naomi's own bedroom. Their love-making had been quick, almost brutal, and very intense. Rachel remembered the massive orgasm she'd had, just brought about by Gordon's virile thrusting inside her, a part of the sex act that usually did not make her come. But on this occasion she had been on fire from the start, definitely excited by the fact that Gordon's wife was possibly nearby but also by the fact that somebody could barge in at any moment and catch them in the act.

After that fiery first encounter, Gordon had come to Rachel's place regularly, their love-making continued to be great, but Rachel kept being disappointed at Gordon's regular disappearances overnight. And she never heard him getting up in the middle of the night, putting on his clothes, probably going to the bathroom, and guiltily tip-toing out of her flat. And yet, she could not let go of

him. At least not for the moment. And her biological clock was ticking …

To distract her from her dark thoughts, Rachel picked up the pile of papers she had brought back from work that lay in front of her on the breakfast table. Not only was she frustrated about how things were going, or not going, with Gordon, but the 'moorboy case' was also frustrating. Rachel looked at forensic scientist Hazel Molfese's latest report on top of the pile. There were a few new developments, but nothing that so far made identification of the boy easier. Hazel now had the full DNA sequence for the boy. Thanks to recent scientific developments it was now possible, and relatively cheap, to obtain the full genetic profile of a victim in a short timescale. But they had so far not been able to match this profile with any living relative. The problem was, of course, that no DNA samples were available for the majority of the population, and that the only comparable DNA samples accessible to forensic scientists at Harbourtown Constabulary were of criminals and other victims. But none of these had shown any match with moorboy. Unless resources were made available to swab ten million people in the south-west of the UK for their genetic profiles, a demand Rachel knew was impossible to make, for the moment at least the DNA evidence led them nowhere.

Rachel glanced at the rest of Hazel's report. Moorboy's hair had been well preserved in the anaerobic conditions of the moor, but the hair colour of the boy was not easily ascertained. Rachel, who was not a forensic expert, was surprised at that. She looked at photos of moorboy appended to Hazel's report that clearly showed well-preserved, matted tufts of hair around the boy's head. On the photo, the boy's hair appeared to be brown-black, but Rachel suspected that this might just be the colour of the peat encrusted in the boy's hair. But reading Hazel's detailed description of the analysis of the boy's hair, Rachel quickly realised that it was not easy to identify the colour of hair of a body that had been buried for a while in peat. She skimmed over Hazel's scientific explanation as to why this was the case, but she was interested in reading that most ancient bog bodies ended up with reddish hair. Somehow the chemistry of the peat changed hair colouring. But Hazel's report said that, as the boy's body was at most about 30 years old, some remnant original hair colour was still detectable. She assumed that the chance that they boy was blond was about 40%, brown-haired 30% and with black or red hair making up the rest. *Not much to go by here either!*, Rachel thought frustrated.

Most frustrating for her was the fact that she still could not build up a mental image of how the boy looked. She knew he was probably thin and lanky,

and possibly blond, but that was about it. Not enough to picture a living kid, playing with his mates and enjoying life before coming to an untimely end. Very frustrating!

While taking a big swig of the deliciously frothy cappuccino made with her superb Italian *Gaggia* coffee machine, Rachel turned to the second report lying in front of her. This had been written for her benefit by Sergeant Inzuman Patel, who she had assigned to scour all databases of missing kids. In the first instance, Inzuman had been told to restrict his investigation to England's south-west, comprising about 10 million inhabitants. Although a large number, this was not an impossible task, as by simple elimination the number of possible missing kids could be whittled down to a reasonable number, or so Rachel had originally thought. Inzuman's meticulously written report – Rachel had not expected anything less from her excellent colleague – started by spelling out the parameters of his search. To be on the safe side, and to include a wide enough margin of error, Inzuman had looked at all unsolved cases involving boys aged 9 to14 in south-west England for the time span 5 to 40 years ago. Inzuman had double-checked with Hazel and she had assured him that, based on the evidence in front of her, moorboy's body could not have been dumped in the moor less than five and more than 40 years ago. Based on the lack of further details about

moorboy in terms of appearance, this, unfortunately still left a lot of disappeared boys to contend with.

Rachel was surprised at the figures Inzuman discussed in his report. Over 120,000 children went missing in the UK every year, which meant nearly 20,000 children disappearing in England's south-west alone! And who was to say that moorboy's body had not come from further afield than the south-west? But they had to start somewhere. This meant 10,000 boys going missing in the south-west every year through kidnapping, neglect, getting lost or just disappearing without a trace. Of these, about 3000 boys per year in the south-west were aged between 9 and 14. Rachel was relieved to see that only about two percent of missing children were long-term missing or never found. Although this was a low figure, Inzuman's report showed that this still translated to 60 boys aged 9 to 14 disappearing long-term every year from south-west England alone. Multiplied by the 35 years spanning their investigation, this meant that Inzuman had over 2000 missing boys in that age range on his list.

Rachel put down her cappuccino. Over 2000 boys! With the manpower, or lack thereof, at Harbourtown Constabulary this would take months, possibly years, to fully investigate!

Rachel read on to see what progress Inzuman had made. Inzuman described how he had worked full-time for the past four days trying to contact

relatives of these missing boys. He had started first with those boys listed missing near Harbourtown, numbering about 300 for the timespan and age range in question, as they still hoped that moorboy was a local boy. First, Inzuman tried to get hold of all police reports filed for these missing boys. As these were held in different constabularies all over England's south-west, Inzuman had so far only been able to see a few dozen, either electronically, or, not unsurprising, many in still not digitised paper form. In his report, Inzuman described how varied the quality of these police reports were: some were very detailed with clear information about the missing boys' appearance and what they had been wearing. But other reports only contained scant information about these details and were almost useless for their specific attempt at matching moorboy with one of these missing boys. Inzuman had highlighted in marker pen his key assessment of these police reports: "If our boy is one based on one of these relatively incomplete reports, then our chances of matching him with one of these missing boys is almost nil."

That does not sound good!, was Rachel's first thought at reading Inzuman's incisive critique of poor police reporting of missing children. Inzuman's report continued by explaining why it was paramount to, therefore, also attempt to contact the families of these missing boys, especially in

cases where the police reports did not provide full detail. Although Inzuman had, so far, only begun to scratch the surface, he nonetheless had made some progress in this regard. So far, Inzuman had been able to contact 12 of the families with local missing boys, but another 13 families had not been contactable with the information they had, and had either moved away, died, or were no longer traceable for other reasons. In many cases, therefore, it would prove almost impossible to supplement the scant information from missing boys' reports with information provided by these boys' families. Rachel sighed. This did not look too promising either.

Inzuman then described the questions he asked the families he had been able to get hold of: first, obviously, whether the missing boy had eventually been found, which was the case in 2 of the 12 contacted families, despite the fact that the respective police report had made no mention of this; second, roughly what height and build their boy was when he disappeared, which clearly discounted another 3 boys, 4 cases were inconclusive, and the remaining 3 missing boys were definite possibles; and, thirdly, whether anyone in the family of the missing boys knew whether their missing boy had been wearing a 'Harvester' kid's XL-size t-shirt at the time of disappearance. Of the seven still in this small

sample of 12 (including the inconclusives), only one person could say with absolute certainty that their boy had never worn 'Harvester' t-shirts, while the others either did not know or said that their boy had been so 'wild', 'unruly' or 'uncontrollable' that he could have worn anything without them knowing about it. At least this latter information tallied with some of the police reports that stated 'no information' under the rubric 'clothing worn at time of disappearance'. But, to Rachel, this lack of information from members of their families about the boy's clothing was also a sad indication of the loose, unloving, or even problematic links some of these families had with their own children.

Rachel put down the report and glanced out of her kitchen window towards her back garden. Her thoughts were briefly distracted by a siskin fluttering about and eventually landing on a birch branch. Rachel loved her flat and especially her back garden and how it attracted birds. The garden was not big, but it was nicely enclosed by a large two-meter-high brick wall that adjoined neighbouring properties, and it had a very sunny south-facing orientation. The front part of the garden comprised a patio made of beautiful black *aluri* limestone the previous owner had put in just before Rachel had moved in, and Rachel had placed some sturdy garden furniture on it that would be less

likely to be blown about in the frequent south-westerly gales that affected Harbourtown regularly.

She loved sitting there in the sun, sipping a cappuccino. A ray of sunshine pierced through the clouds as they raced through the sky, pushed by the usual strong south-westerly, and lit up part of Rachel's kitchen: bunches of dried herbs hung on the wall, glistened in the sunshine, and swayed gently in the hot air current; racks of pickles, jams and marmalades that glinted in the sunlight; Rachel's prized French terracotta cooking set on a shelf along the wall which refracted the rays of the sun; and her assorted pot plants on the windowsill that were bathed in the warm sunshine. For a short moment, moorboy and Gordon seemed miles away …

But inevitably Rachel's thoughts took her back to Inzuman's report. Although the report clearly suggested that some progress could be made with regard to the list of missing boys, especially if Inzuman focused first on missing local boys, it would probably still take Inzuman about two months full-time work just to go through the list of local boys, and even then probably only about half of these would yield any meaningful facts. Although worth pursuing other police files reporting the disappearances and additional information from the boys' families, clearly they had to find additional ways to identify moorboy.

They had discussed a local newspaper campaign asking the general population for information, but the problem there was that so few people now read the local newspaper that the *Harbourtown Herald* had gone bust three years ago. There was no longer a local paper in Harbourtown! They already used the Constabulary *Facebook* and *Twitter* accounts to divulge information about the fact that they were seeking help to identify the body of a boy found on the moor, and south-west BBC news had broadcast a brief clip about the discovery of moorboy's body but, from past experience, Rachel did not expect much useful resonance from the public in this respect.

It was frustrating, and to Rachel it was clear that they had to explore the DNA avenue further. But first of all, Rachel had to get ready for her first EIPT meeting in Paris in two days' time. Second, she had to find the courage to break up with Gordon and sort out her love life, but that was a different matter altogether. With a sigh Rachel stood up and put the dirty dishes in the sink. Today, she would help Inzuman both to scrutinise further missing boys reports and to call unfortunate families whose boys had disappeared in the past few decades.

10

20 years ago

Kevin found out that the name of the 11-year-old blond boy two years below him at school was Markus Schlesinger. He was German and only spoke broken English. Apparently he just lived with his dad who had a 'secondment' – at age 14 Kevin did not know what that word meant – at the Harbourtown military base. He had heard that it had something to do with technical advice about the nuclear submarines based at Harbourtown. Kevin now understood why Markus had been shunned by his schoolmates: they taunted him for being German, for being a 'Nazi', for not speaking English properly, and for being blond and blue-eyed just like the baddies in B-rated second world war movies. But it was precisely these latter attributes that attract Kevin to the boy, the way he looked, his slightly demure and shy attitude.

Kevin had surreptitiously observed Markus for a few weeks. Armoured with his newfound knowledge as to why Markus always stood apart from his school mates, Kevin had finally mustered the courage one day and had approached the boy at

the edge of the school yard. First he had made sure that they could not be overseen by other kids.

"Hi, what's your name?", Kevin asked as he awkwardly approached Markus who had been lost in thought and had not seen the bigger boy approach.

Markus looked up. What did this older boy want from him? More taunts about his German-ness, about his accent, about the fact that he was different? Markus glanced around him to see whether other boys were nearby, but the older boy seemed to be on his own. The older boy almost seemed a bit lost and nervous.

"I am Kevin", Kevin said to Markus. "I'm in year nine."

"I am Markus", the German boy replied shyly with a high-pitched pre-pubescent voice.

"Would you like to meet up after school and play?", Kevin asked. In his imagination, he had thought long and hard about how he could lure the German boy away from school after class, and had arrived at the conclusion that this direct approach was the only one that made sense. No point in beating about the bush! He wanted to be alone with Markus. Just standing next to the slim blond boy got Kevin aroused.

Markus glanced around him nervously. He was not at all sure what to make of this sudden invitation by an older boy. But then Kevin seemed OK, he was

rather small and thin like Markus himself and did not look like much of a threat. And Markus' father would be out working late again which meant that Markus would just, as usual, hang around their spacious flat on his own, not knowing what to do.

"Yes, sure", Markus replied with a hint of a smile. In many ways he was proud that he was finally being approached in a friendly way by one of the kids at school, and an older kid at that.

"That's great", Kevin replied, visibly relieved at how easy this had been. "Let's meet at the northern gate at the end of class. We could go up to the moor or somethin' …?"

"Sure, that sounds great. I'll see you then … Kevin", Markus said, although he was not quite sure whether Kevin meant the large hill area called 'Devonmoor' that arose just behind their school and that comprised large areas of grassland, woods and peat bogs. He had always been curious about the moor but had not dared explore it by himself.

Kevin was very pleased with himself. His encounter with Markus had gone better than he could have hoped for in his wildest dreams. Somehow he had envisaged resistance and belligerence by the German boy, but Markus seemed keen to meet him and go with him to the moor. But as he sat in his next class, boring French, Kevin also felt increasingly nervous now that his long-hatched plan was becoming reality. Would he

be able to overpower Markus and do to him what he planned to do? Was this really what he wanted? But his sexual urge was too strong. His throbbing erection – thankfully concealed from his classmates by Kevin's school desk – confirmed that it was time. Time to be in control of his own body for the first time since Keith last raped him years ago, time to be in control over somebody else for a change.

But time on the wall clock seemed to crawl like treacle, Kevin kept staring at it all the time. He could not wait to see Markus. Hopefully Markus would not change his mind and get cold feet last minute, Kevin thought in despair, anxiously chewing his fingernails. Finally, the last lesson was finished. Kevin quickly gathered his school stuff and made his way to the north entrance of the school. Relieved, Kevin saw that Markus stood by the gate, hands in the pockets of his school trousers, his white school shirt and a cream-coloured t-shirt both half hanging out of his trousers and his tie dangling untidily from his neck. Markus waved timidly as he saw Kevin approach.

"Hi Markus", Kevin said and put his arm around the German boy's thin shoulders. "Let's go then …", and both boys made their way through the last row of houses and up a path that led to the moor.

As they made their way up the slope, past gorse bushes and avoiding patches of wet peat, Markus tried to make conversation by asking Kevin

questions about school and Harbourtown, but Kevin was rather tight-lipped and only gave cursory replies. He did not want to put off Markus, so he politely gave short answers to satisfy the young boy's curiosity, but he had other things on his mind. He had to stay focused on what he was about to do to Markus.

But, as they continued their way up the slope on a less-well marked path, Kevin had to admit that he did not quite know what his plan actually was. He had not expected Markus to agree to come with him so quickly and on that very day, which had left Markus with no time to better scout out the area. Although Kevin knew this part of the moor a little bit – from the odd lonely foray he had undertaken on his own after school – he had never been on the path they were on. Although the path looked rough and not often frequented by other people, Kevin did not know where it led and whether it would be appropriate for what he was about to do to Markus.

Kevin stopped and glanced around him. Both boys panted as they had made their way up the hill relatively quickly. They both turned around and looked down towards Harbourtown, stretching out below them, the military shipyard by the estuary clearly visible in the distance, the sea a shimmering silvery glimmer on the horizon, the sprawl of Harbourtown hospital and the adjacent industrial park to their right, and their school surrounded by

one of the poorest and most ramshackle suburbs of Harbourtown just below them. Viewed from above, the school – one of the largest in Harbourtown – looked tiny and far away.

"We'll just go a bit further", Kevin said, looking at Markus who seemed less and less sure about whether it had been a good idea to join the older boy on this walk through the moor. It was evident that Markus had not envisaged them going for a hike, but had rather thought that they would stay somewhere just on the outskirts of the moor and play. But Markus did not want to show the older boy that he was a bit afraid, and he followed Kevin who had taken the lead again and walked up the slope briskly.

After a short while Kevin stopped near a large gorse bush with a grassy area next to it that was not too boggy. He glanced around him to make sure nobody else was around and that they could not be seen from below. This was it! This was the moment of truth! This was the test whether he could do it! Without hesitating he suddenly grabbed Markus by the arm and pulled him to the ground. At first Markus thought that this was a game Kevin wanted to play, but he quickly realised that Kevin's demeanour had changed. Kevin looked like a different person, his expression stony-faced and dour, his stare expressionless and robotic. Kevin was now very aroused and his stiff penis was clearly

visible through his school trousers. Markus stared at the bulge and did not know what to make of it. At his age, he did not understand what was going on. He tried to wrestle himself free from Markus' stranglehold, but, being much smaller, he had no chance against the bigger boy. "Let me go!", Markus shrieked. "I want to go home now!"

But it was too late. It was as if another personality had taken hold of Kevin. With strength he did not know he possessed, Kevin tore off Markus school jacket and tie and ripped open Markus' shirt. He then, with difficulty, yanked off the boy's t-shirt, exposing the German boy's thin and pale chest. This aroused Kevin even more. He opened Markus' leather belt with one hand while pushing down hard on the German boy's naked chest with his other. Markus was now putting up a real fight and screamed. Kevin put his hand on Markus' mouth and glared at him menacingly: "If you don't shut up I'll kill you! Do you hear?"

Markus nodded, fear in his eyes and tears streaking down his cheeks. He went all limp and stopped struggling. He realised that he could not overpower Kevin.

In the meantime, Kevin had opened his own belt and zipper and had begun pulling down his trousers. This was awkward as he still had his shoes on, and even in his frenzied and maniac state Kevin realised that he had not thought about such details when he

had played through in his mind over-and-over again in the past few days how his rape of Markus would unfold. But somehow he managed to yank off his shoes while still holding down Markus, which was easier now that he sat astride Markus' pelvis. Kevin pulled down his own underpants and exposed his erect penis. Markus stared at it with utter fear in his eyes. Only now did he realise what was going to happen.

"Touch it!", Kevin screamed, leading Markus' hand towards his penis.

Markus was repulsed at touching Kevin's erection, but he had no other choice. He knew that he was in grave danger. Kevin made Markus move his hand up and down on his penis. Kevin closed his eyes. He liked being touched by somebody else. Anyone, just not his own hands! Images of Keith lying on top of him, inside him, flashed up in his mind. Kevin brushed these thoughts away. This was about him, not Keith! He was in control now! He would do to somebody else what Keith had done to him!

Kevin pulled down Markus' trousers with his free hand. Still sitting astride on Markus' pelvis, he took off Markus shoes and pulled Markus' trousers over his feet. He pulled down Markus' underpants, which revealed Markus' small, white and limp penis. In his mind, Kevin had envisaged Markus being aroused by what he did, a huge erection

thrusting towards him. But reality was different and Kevin was very disappointed at Markus' lack of sexual response. He began stroking Markus' penis. Markus had given up all attempts at fighting back, just lay limply on his back, and let Kevin touch him. Markus had his head turned sideways, tears streaking down his cheeks. He did not want to look at what Kevin did to him.

After a while of futile stroking, Kevin gave up trying to arouse the German boy. This was certainly not how he had imagined it! Angrily, he turned Markus around and forced him to kneel in front of him. With both his hands Kevin parted Markus' small buttocks and glared at the boy's anus. Violently, Kevin pushed his erect Penis into Markus. Markus cried out in pain. Markus' anus was tight, very tight, much tighter than Kevin had imagined in his visions of the rape. The memory of the searing pain he had experienced himself when Keith had raped him briefly overwhelmed him. Again, Kevin brushed aside these thoughts. *I'm in control, I'm in control ...* he made himself think while pushing his penis deeper inside Markus. But Kevin could feel Markus' sphincter muscle tighten, almost squeezing out Kevin's penis.

"If you don't relax I'm going to kill you!", Kevin shouted, putting one hand around Markus' throat.

Markus was now sobbing loudly, but he somehow managed to relax enough so that Kevin could push his penis deeper inside. While thrusting deeper and faster, Kevin stroked Markus' penis with one hand, still hoping for an erection. But Markus stayed limp, too scared and in too much pain to be able to get aroused.

Markus increased the cadence of his thrusts, he felt great now: fully in control, very aroused and dominant. He could feel the slow onset of his orgasm, the mounting pleasure, as he felt Markus' penis with his left hand and while staring at his own penis moving in and out of Markus anus, the German boy's skinny back, and Markus' slim buttocks moving in unison with Kevin's rhythmic thrusts. Kevin's orgasm was like a massive explosion, seemingly endless and beautifully intense. Apart from his uncontrollable wet dreams, this was his first orgasm since Keith had jerked him off so many years ago. With the last spasms of Kevin's orgasm abating, his thrusting inside Markus slowed down and then stopped altogether.

For Kevin, it was if he suddenly woke up, the world around him suddenly coming back into focus. For the first time in a while he could hear Markus whimpering below him, the sounds of the moor with the wind playing with the gorse and some distant bird screeching; the smell of the peaty soil underneath them; the wet-moist fragrance of the

vegetation around them; the tickle of the dappled sunlight trying to break through the grey clouds rushing over their heads.

Kevin held Markus' buttocks with both his hands, these beautiful small and skinny buttocks that had turned him on so much. He let his now limp penis slide out of Markus' and just stayed there, kneeling behind Markus for a few seconds. As soon as Kevin had slid out of Markus, the German boy collapsed onto the ground, crying loudly. "Daddy! I want my daddy!", he sobbed, lying face-down in the peat, his head in his hands.

The reality of the situation suddenly hit Kevin. What had he done? He had just raped a young boy! It was almost as if Kevin looked down onto himself from a birds-eye-view, down onto the scene in front of him with himself kneeling above the naked and frail body of whimpering Markus. It was at this point that Kevin realised that he could not let Markus live. But in his mind, he had never played out the last part of the act. The invoking of the rape in his mind had always stopped with his orgasm – and that of Markus – but had never gone beyond that point. In his mind it had all just been about sexual gratification, about being able to have an erection, about somebody else touching his penis, about using another boy's body to reach orgasm. It had never been about what would happen next.

Markus of course knew Kevin's name, he knew he was a boy in year nine from the same school. There was no way that Kevin would get away with this if he let Markus live.

While Markus still lay face down in the peat, whimpering and calling for his dad, Kevin grabbed Markus' leather belt. He lifted Markus' head slightly – there was no resistance from the German boy – and placed the leather belt around Markus' throat, closing the belt loop at the back of the neck. Kevin then pulled hard on the bit sticking out from the loop, which immediately tightened the belt around Markus' neck. Markus panicked and began struggling hard. While Kevin further tightened the belt around Markus' neck, Markus tried to stop him with flailing arms and hands, but, being pinned down by Kevin sitting on Markus' pelvis with all his weight, the German boy never had a chance. After a short while he stopped struggling, and a few seconds later Markus' body went completely limp. Kevin held the stranglehold for another 20 seconds or so, making sure the German boy was definitely dead.

He had felt nothing while killing Markus. He knew it had to be done, that was just it! One small part of his revenge for what Keith had done to him, for taking away his youth, his sexuality, all the pleasures in life, for making him a freak!

Kevin stood up, carefully glancing around him to see whether anyone was in the vicinity. But the moor around them was empty, nobody was around. He quickly put his clothes and shoes back on. But his lack of forward planning became even more evident now. Ho to dispose of the body? He had no shovel or any other implement with which to dig a hole in which to discard the body. But he also could not leave the body near the path. So he carried Markus' naked and limp body about 20 metres further up the hill, not worrying about the leather belt still around the boy's neck. Having found the wettest and boggiest patch in the vicinity, Kevin began digging the ground with his bare hands. He found it surprisingly easy to dig deep down without encountering any roots or stones, and after only about 15 minutes he had dug out a hole that was big enough for Markus' body to fit in. He went back down to the site of the rape and grabbed Markus' clothes which he then tossed into the hole next to Markus' body. It took him only a few minutes to cover Markus' remains with a mound of wet peat. He then trampled down the earth as best he could, and after a while he was pleased with his work: with the muddy and wet ground everywhere around him, it was almost impossible to tell that a body lay buried underneath. Hopefully, Markus' body would never be found.

It was with very mixed emotions that Kevin made his way back down the slope. His trousers, shirt and school jacket were covered in mud and peat, he would need to find a good excuse to explain this to his mum! But he also felt a strange feeling of elation, like a giant weight had been taken off his shoulders. What he had done was exactly what he needed. He was hooked, and he certainly did not feel bad about having taken somebody's life. On the contrary, he felt in full control. For the first time in years he felt happy. But he also felt slightly annoyed at himself. His imagination before the rape and murder had got the better of him, the rape of Markus had not been well planned at all, Markus' body had not responded the way he had imagined it would, and he knew that he had been lucky that Markus had acceded so quickly to come with him to the moor in the first place. He would have to be better prepared next time.

11

The present

Stefan Scholz seemed like a nice enough guy. At first, Rachel was unsure whether she should join his invitation to come to dinner at the posh-sounding Parisian restaurant *La cage du Roi Louis*, but she was pleased to see that the restaurant exuded the typical French charm of excellent food, served by friendly waiters, but also a relatively relaxed atmosphere without dress code or pretentions that often marred Rachel's few restaurant outings back home in so-called 'posh' Harbourtown restaurants.

Rachel and Stefan had settled into their comfortably padded mock-18th century chairs, that mirrored the Louis XIV theme of the restaurant, and were perusing the menu. It had been a busy first day at the EIPT meeting in Paris, but Rachel had enjoyed every minute. The meeting was held at the headquarters of *Interpol Europe* located in one of the skyscrapers of the quartier of *La Défense*, Paris' 1970s answer to the modernist planning wave that had swept most West European capitals. *La Défense* had reminded Rachel of London's slightly later modernist and austere *Canary Wharf* development, but she had to admit that the large room on the top

floor where the meeting was held had one of the most stunning urban views she had ever seen, with the whole city of Paris stretching out seemingly endlessly in front of them, with the iconic *Tour Eiffel* and *Arc de Triomphe* just barely visible in the distance through the hazy urban pollution.

"So, what did you make of your first EIPT day?", Stefan Scholz asked, taking Rachel out of her reverie.

Rachel glanced back at Stefan over the rim of her menu. She was unsure whether she found Stefan attractive, with his short-cropped hair, his stylish rimless glasses and his semi-casual tieless attire typical for many Germans professionals. But his face looked kind and she liked his smile, which exuded a child-like innocence. She guessed that Stefan was maybe in his early 40s and wondered whether he was married.

"I really enjoyed it", Rachel replied. "I had feared that it would be rather dull and technical, but I was surprised at how much we actually covered on this first day." What Rachel did not want to admit to Stefan was that she did not get on at all with her British colleague Brian Bambridge, her British counterpart on the EIPT team. Right from the start, Brian had turned out to be a complete asshole, one of these typical pompous Brits who thought that they were better than their European colleagues, who spoke with a posh accent that made them sound

more like idiots than sophisticated people, and who felt utterly entitled to be there in the first place. Rachel thought that Bambridge was almost certainly a Brexiter, although she had to admit that this should have nothing to do with how she assessed a fellow colleague on the EIPT committee. But, still, she hated Brexiters with their narrow-minded bigoted view of the world who still did not want to admit that Britain was going down the drain even faster than before due to the now persistent lack of skilled immigrants and the cutting of economic ties with the EU as Britain's largest trading partner. Although Rachel had drifted towards the only other Brit in the room initially, it had taken her only a few seconds of talking to this pompous bigot to decide to sit somewhere else.

When Rachel sat as far away as possible from Bambridge, on the last available empty seat next to Stefan Scholz, Bambridge gave her a nasty stare which clearly implied that he already saw her as a traitor to the British EIPT cause. In her brief chat with Bambridge, Rachel had not even gone as far as to ascertain what Bambridge's agenda was on the EIPT, but she was sure that she would do everything to torpedo this pompous ass' suggestions whenever she could. But she also hoped that her belligerent stance would not backfire back home, and she was particularly unsure how quickly knowledge of this early rift in the 'British EIPT team' would filter

back to superintendent Warrington in Harbourtown or, even worse, to the Home Office in London. But then, Rachel thought while occasionally glancing back at Bambridge during the meeting, she had to follow her gut instinct when it came to people, an instinct which had always served her well so far. And she had certainly enjoyed chatting to Stefan Scholz during the meeting, whose English had proven to be absolutely fluent. Like many Brits, Rachel was amazed at how many Europeans had English as their second language, especially compared to most British people who, despite years of German, Spanish or French at school, could not even utter a simple sentence in these languages.

"I must admit", Rachel continued her chat with Stefan while glancing at the menu, and happy to put thoughts about Bambridge behind her for the moment, "that I had not expected the remit of the EIPT to be so far-ranging."

Stefan glanced back at her with a smile. "That's exactly what I thought after my first EIPT meeting two years ago", he replied, already answering one of the questions Rachel had on her mind. Stefan was obviously already relatively experienced with EIPT meetings and would be a good source of information.

"But I was also surprised at how much time was actually spent on discussing counter-terrorism issues, rather than what I would call nitty-gritty

policing matters", Rachel said while taking a first sip of the *Beaujolais* wine they had ordered, and that had just been decanted by a white-wigged and waist-coated waiter whose clothes and demeanour perfectly matched the restaurant's 18th-century theme. The wine was excellent.

"Yes, that comes as a surprise to many newcomers to EIPT", Stefan replied. "Although the main remit of the new *European International Police Taskforce* is to improve international and cross-border crime-solving collaboration in general, unfortunately these days this means having also to look at counter-terrorism measures, as recent attacks have yet again proven that counter-terrorism and combating cross-border crime go hand-in-hand. But I thought that we also covered a lot of issues not directly related to terrorism today."

Stefan was right. Rachel had been particularly interested in the afternoon session that involved examples of crime case studies that showed how the *lack* of international collaboration in the past had led to long and protracted national investigations, where cases could have been solved much more quickly had at least some collaboration occurred across borders. These cases mainly involved serial killers who had operated in more than one country and had used similar methods to kill their victims. But the case studies presented clearly showed that in most cases national police forces had lacked the

information to tie different murders together, and that they were too often narrowly focused on their own backyards, rather than seeing wider patterns that showed evident parallels between cases across different countries and police jurisdictions. One of the presenters had referred to this as 'linkage blindness' where national police forces could not associate crimes across different jurisdictions. Worst of all, the shrewdest criminals precisely exploited this linkage blindness by choosing locations for their evil deeds across different jurisdictions. It was partly to address issues of linkage blindness that EIPT had been created.

"What role does *Interpol* play in all this?", Rachel asked Stefan as they tucked into their delicious *pavé de boef* with sautéed potatoes and perfectly seasoned broccoli and asparagus.

"*Interpol* is basically the overarching international agency, of which EIPT is a subset", Stefan explained. "*Interpol* are the ones who do the 'hands-on' work, i.e. coordinating warrants, mobilising *Interpol* agents who have the right to arrest suspects anywhere in Europe and beyond, and, most importantly, managing data and information flow. The latter occurs in the building in *La Défense* where we were today, the headquarters of *Interpol Europe*. That's the main thing these guys do: number crunching, going through thousands of police files in different

languages, coordinating crime information across jurisdictions. We at EIPT are just a talking shop compared to the guys at *Interpol*, and I guess that we focus on the big picture, such as wider strategies. But most importantly, and as you will have been informed by your Home Office, we report back to our own respective countries about this international crime-solving collaboration, the latest trends, the latest big cases, and so on. So, it is important what we do, although it is unlikely that we will be involved with the real hands-on of solving international crimes. That is still the remit of *Interpol* and national police forces."

Rachel was grateful for Stefan's explanations. Although she had been briefed by the Home Office about her role in EIPT, the actual detail of how EIPT fitted in with what *Interpol* did had not been fully explained to her. But she now also realised that, whether she wanted it or not, she probably would have to collaborate with this pompous idiot Bambridge when they reported back to the Home Office. She would just have to swallow her pride and be as professional as she could. But she shuddered just thinking about how repulsive she had found her UK colleague.

"Beyond EIPT, what are the big cases happening in Germany at the moment?", Rachel asked, trying to glean more information about what Stefan was working on.

"I work for the Nürnberg – sorry Nuremberg in English – police force where I am in charge of the homicide division", Stefan replied while scraping the last spoon-full of lemon sorbet ice cream with a dash of mint from his dessert bowl. They had finished the bottle of wine and had moved on to a beautifully mellow, sweet and almondy *Di Saronno* liquor which went very well with the ice cream. Rachel wondered how high up Stefan was in the German police hierarchy, but being 'in charge' of a division implied that he was probably more like Superintend Warrington, i.e. a bit higher in the ranks than Rachel. But Rachel did not mind that. At least Stefan had not boasted about his police career and that he was probably a high-flyer like most people on the EIPT committee, even including people like Bambridge Rachel had to grudgingly admit.

"I deal with a wide range of cases", Stefan continued, "from family homicides to gang violence, the latter of which is fortunately rare in Nürnberg, to, in theory at least, serial killers. But the last serial killer in our area dates back to Kuno Hofmann in 1972, the 'vampire of Nürnberg', who killed several people, committed necrophilia and, apparently, drank the blood of his dead victims. But this was well before my time and probably not the most appropriate discussion topic over a sorbet …" Stefan raised his liquor glass and smiled at Rachel.

She had not flinched when he had mentioned the gruesome story of Hofmann, which encouraged him to continue. "But about a year ago we had a very sad case of an 11-year old boy raped and killed in the Nürnberg district of Schönwalde, a poor area near the airport. Although we have the DNA of the sadistic perpetrator, at the moment we still have no clues as to who he is or where we could find him. I think this case will continue to preoccupy me for quite a while …"

Rachel looked back at him. "Interestingly, we at Harbourtown Constabulary … in the south-west of England", Rachel quickly interjected the latter bit of geographical information, fully aware that most Europeans had probably never heard of middle-sized Harbourtown, "are also currently investigating the murder of an 11-year-old boy. What a coincidence!"

Stefan seemed interested, and, as they sipped their cappuccinos to round up what had been a delicious meal, Rachel filled in Stefan about moorboy's case, how the body had been discovered, the possible date of the murder, the few clues they had, the fact that they also had DNA from the body itself but could not match it with anyone in their missing boys records, and the frustration they were experiencing with the case.

"You see, these types of cases are precisely what EIPT should be about", Stefan said more

jokingly than earnest. "To join the dots of disparate cases in different jurisdictions together, for colleagues from different countries to speak to each other about similar cases."

But they both knew that it was just coincidence that they were both working on the murder of young boys, as the cases were evidently very different, with one being recent while the other dated back 10 to 30 years ago. They quickly moved on to more cheerful chatter. Rachel found out that Stefan was 43 years old, that he had been married but was now divorced, that he had two boys aged 9 and 11, who lived with their mum, who he only saw every second weekend. Stefan mentioned that he struggled a bit with the fact that one of his latest murder victims was about the same age as his oldest son, and that he had felt even more protective of his children since the investigation had started. But he also felt that he could not fully protect his two boys as he only saw them once a fortnight. Rachel could clearly depict some bitterness in Stefan's account about how he felt slightly disassociated from his two sons, and that he was a bit frustrated with his life overall at the moment. Stefan even mentioned that he thought about changing career, which Rachel found strange considering how professional Stefan's approach appeared to be at the EIPT meeting and how passionately he had talked about his job.

Rachel in turn had not revealed much about herself. She had told Stefan that she was single, but she certainly avoided mentioning Gordon and her predicament regarding her rather unsatisfying recent flings with married men. As they both paid their separate bills and left *La cage du Roi Louis*, she was still not entirely sure whether she wanted to pass the night with Stefan. Had he sent out vibes that he was interested in her? But when they took a taxi together and he put his arm around her, Rachel's hesitation vanished. Although they had originally intended for the taxi to drop her off at her hotel first, and then for Stefan to continue on to where he was staying, they both got out at Rachel's hotel.

12

16 months ago

The workshop at Geneva University was over. Kevin had been relieved that it had finished in a very Swiss-like manner exactly on time at 2pm on the third day, just as the workshop timetable had suggested. This had meant that he did not have to leave the meeting early to make it in time by bus to the suburb of Clemenceau to do 'it', before catching his flight back to Bristol at 7.15pm.

After catching a perfectly-on-time bus – not a taxi as the driver would be able to remember a passenger being ferried to what was to become a crime scene – Kevin took up his position behind the garages in the same spot he had scouted out two days earlier. The dishevelled housing estate built in the 1970s or 1980s stretched out all around him, and, just like two days ago, plenty of kids were running around unattended in the rubbish-strewn playground in front of the garages. Nobody seemed to have spotted him or had paid any attention to him as he had walked to his spot past the towering social housing blocks. Kevin was relieved to see that the same 11- or 12-year-old boy he had seen two days ago, possibly of Pakistani origin, was again

forlornly kicking a football against the garage doors, a bit apart from a bunch of younger kids playing in the playground. Kevin knew from past experience that he was lucky, as it was not always guaranteed that he would catch a boy on his own, especially one he had already scouted out earlier and, most importantly, whose appearance he liked. Indeed, his window of opportunity was always rather narrow, as he had a plane to catch and sometimes in the past he'd had to make do with whatever boy he could find. But not this time!

Kevin peeked out from behind the garages to make sure that no adults were watching. He was not bothered about the younger kids playing nearby as they were too young to make good witnesses, even if the police asked them later. When he was satisfied that nobody else was around and that no cars were approaching the garages, he broke cover and walked towards the Pakistani boy. Kevin liked the appearance of the boy: he was very slim and lanky and looked more like 11-years-old than 12 or 13, which suited Kevin perfectly. And if the boy was indeed from Pakistan or possibly India, it was also likely that he spoke English, as Kevin's command of French was not good enough to hold a lengthy introductory conversation in French. As he had done so many times before, Kevin held out a banknote to the boy, this time a red-and-blue 20 Swiss Francs note.

"Bonjour, mon petit. Est-ce que tu parles Anglais?", Kevin asked nonchalantly in broken French and with a pretty bad accent.

The boy nodded and replied: "Yes, I speak English".

The boy's voice had clearly not broken yet, which confirmed to Kevin that he was about right with his estimation of the boy's age of about 11.

"Would you like to earn some money?", Kevin asked with his usual casual tone and holding the banknote right in front of the boy's face. How often had he had tried this strategy, and how often had he been able to lure boys away with just the wave of a banknote!

The boy stared back at Kevin with large brown eyes, evidently unsure what to do, and glanced back at one of the housing blocks.

"My mum says that I should not talk to strangers …", the boy said shyly.

Hmmmm. I hope he will not cause any problems!, Kevin thought, getting annoyed at the boy's hesitation. *Maybe people look after their kids in this area after all! Obviously somebody has talked to him about 'stranger danger'!*

Kevin glanced in the direction in which the boy was looking, but the block of flats was too far away to make out any detail. In turn, anyone watching from the flats would also be too far away to make

out exactly what was happening in front of the garages.

"I have a box over there which is a bit too heavy for me to carry to my car. Look, I pay you 20 Swiss Francs just for one minute of your time to help me to carry that box", Kevin said in an alluring voice as possible.

The boy had evidently understood what Kevin said. The boy's eyes flitted to-and-fro from Kevin's face to the red-and-blue banknote dangling in front of his eyes. Kevin thought that he detected a brief glimmer of greed in the boy's eyes and, after a few seconds, knew that the boy was hooked. Twenty Swiss Francs, about the same as €20, was a fortune for any kid that age, especially in this deprived neighbourhood. As Kevin had rightly suspected, with a last glance towards the block of flats, the boy grabbed the banknote out of Kevin's hand, stuffed it into the pocket of his grubby shorts, and followed Kevin towards the back of the garages. While they walked the short distance, Kevin glanced at the young kids playing in the playground and was satisfied to see that they were so preoccupied with their game that they did not look towards him and the Pakistani boy. Kevin led the boy behind the garages and immediately grabbed the boy's arm and held him tight.

I'm not able to help with this.

even further, and then the boy suddenly ejaculated, his penis rhythmically spewing out small amounts of sperm. Kevin, still inside the boy, was amazed that he could feel the boy's orgasmic convulsions through the rhythmic tightening of the boy's anus, and he felt the boy's rapid and moist breath against the palm of his right hand, while the boy reluctantly moaned with pleasure in Kevin's tight embrace

Finally the boy went limp, and Kevin extricated his penis from the boy's anus. But Kevin was so amazed at what had just happened that he hesitated with the next step. Different from other times, where he had been in his usual trance-like state while raping a boy, on this occasion he had been completely lucid the whole time, enjoying and witnessing every second of the boy's arousal and orgasm. But this meant that, this time, he was linked to the Pakistani boy in a way he had never experienced before. The boy had not just been an object for Kevin's depraved lust who could easily be killed, but, in Kevin's warped mind, a strange connection between him and the boy had been established. After all, the boy had come for Kevin! The boy had been aroused by what Kevin had done to him and had even moaned with supressed pleasure!

Tears began streaming down Kevin's face. He could not do it! He could not kill this boy who he had just wonderful sex with. A boy who had come!

For a brief moment, Kevin released his right arm's stranglehold around the boy's neck. Immediately the boy wiggled himself free, and it was only at last second, and as an instinctive reaction, that Kevin managed to grab hold of the boy's right hand. But this brief moment was enough to destroy the intimate link that had built up in Kevin's mind between himself and the boy. It was as if the boy's attempt at escape had catapulted Kevin back into reality, as if Kevin was sucked back from a dream-like state into the present, standing there behind garages in grubby Clemenceau and holding a naked boy in his arms who he had just raped and who tried to escape. Kevin quickly pulled the boy towards him, put his right arm around the boy's neck and applied ever increasing pressure around the boy's throat. With both his hands the boy tried to free himself from Kevin's stranglehold, but he had no chance against an adult. After about 30 seconds, the boy's wriggling and choking sounds abated and he slumped limply into Kevin's arms. The boy was dead.

Kevin let the boy's frail body fall to the ground. The boy's naked body suddenly looked tiny, lying in front of Kevin in the rubbish-strewn dirt, like a small vulnerable animal, like road kill. Kevin glanced around him. Suddenly all the noises his trance-like state had cut out came rushing back. He could hear the noises of the kids playing in the

nearby playground, leaves rustling on a nearby tree, cars could be heard somewhere in the distance. But other than that it was eerily quiet, and Kevin could feel both his heart beating fast and the staccato of his breath pounding against his chest. He quickly pulled up his underpants and trousers, went with his hand through his dishevelled hair, adjusted his shirt, and walked through the bushes away from the garages, not glancing back at the small dead body lying in the dirt. As he emerged onto another garage forecourt he glanced around him to make sure nobody was nearby, and, when he was satisfied that he was alone, he made his way briskly out of the housing estate towards one of the nearby bus stops. The journey to Clemenceau and the rape and murder of the Pakistani boy had lasted less than 90 minutes. He had plenty of time to make it to the airport on time. As Kevin sat in the bus, he hummed a tune and played every second of his own and the boy's orgasms through his mind over-and-over again. He knew that his lust – this unsatiable, uncontrollable, wonderful and awful, all-comprising and overwhelming sexual lust that he could not satisfy on his own – was satiated for a few months at least …

13

The present

Pascal was lying in bed. He had been asleep, but a loud bang had woken him up. He sat up in bed in the dark and listened out for further noises. His alarm clock showed that it was just past midnight. For a while he heard nothing, but then a loud stomping could be heard. His father, Simon, was approaching his room, his heavy footsteps clearly audible on the wooden floor of their small flat. Simon barged into Pascal's bedroom and flicked on the light. Pascal saw immediately that Simon was completely drunk, his acne-scarred face red, his body swaying from side-to-side.

"Nathalie has told me … what you've been up to … at school … hick!", Simon stammered and slurred with his heavy Provençale accent.

Pascal was scared. He thought his father had learned his lesson last time when the two of them had a confrontation, and that the uncomfortable truce between them would last. But Simon was evidently not in a fit state to remember anything. He barged forward, almost fell over some of Pascal's toys on the floor, and landed heavily on Pascal's bed.

"I will teach you to hurt other kids with your … with your … fucking skill … you weirdo!", Simon slurred, raising his first towards Pascal's face.

Although Pascal had sworn to himself not to use his strange gift any more against his parents, his father left him no choice. Simon was about to beat him up. Pascal closed his eyes and concentrated his mind. Like before, when he applied his mind-sucking skills, it felt as if a point in his brain caught fire, as if something inside his head ignited, as if a tiny spot of energy built up and grew inside his forehead, all of which happened in the fraction of a second. He stared at Simon's raised fist, at his father's grotesque red and swollen face, he could smell the man's fetid alcoholic stench. Pascal focused all his energy on Simon's head. Immediately the now familiar shiny yellowish filament emanated from Pascal's forehead, winding its way towards Simon's forehead. Simon's raised fist slowed down as if in slow motion and then froze completely. Simon, who had experienced all this before but had forgotten it in his drunken stupor, stared astonished at the wriggling filament that was about to enter his forehead. Simon winced as the filament grew thicker, it was now a yellow radiating stream of light flickering between Pascal's and Simon's foreheads. Simon tried to touch the filament with his hand, but his fingers just passed through the stream of light, dissipating it into tiny

sparkling fragments that immediately reassembled as if by magic. Simon put a hand to his forehead and moaned in agony. First he fell on his side onto Pascal's bed, but the weight of his lower body then dragged his body down onto the floor where he collapsed in a tangled mass of lifeless limbs. Pascal knew he should stop his mind-sucking, but he was so enraged at his drunken father that he intensified the energy stream with his mind. Although Simon was already unconscious, Pascal could feel his mind probing the deepest recesses of Simon's mind. A reddish, blood-coloured substance was beginning to be sucked out of Simon's forehead. Pascal's mind-sucking was evidently causing harm inside Simon's brain.

Pascal was now in a frenzy. He further intensified the pressure on Simon's head, the yellow radiating stream of light growing stronger. His father had now turned blue in the face and was evidently dying. Suddenly Pascal's door burst open and Nathalie, Pascal's mother, barged in, crying out loud and holding her head in her hands, utterly terrified. A large bloody gash was visible on her forehead, probably the result of Simon's earlier assault that had woken up Pascal.

"Pascal! No! Stop it! You are killing your father!"

In his mind-sucking frenzy, Pascal barely heard his mother. She sounded like a distant voice coming

to him through thick fog. His mind was completely concentrated on sucking out the last remnants of Simon's soul. He was intent on utterly destroying his father. It was only when Nathalie shook Pascal violently, screaming at him, that Pascal realised what was happening. He immediately severed the mental link to his father's mind, the translucid yellow stream of light collapsed, the last yellowish filaments dissipated into thin air.

Pascal had awoken out of his frenzied trance and stared at his mum with abject fear in his eyes. Then he looked down at Simon's lifeless body. He had killed his father, he realised in horror. He had lost control over his skill, and the mind-sucking had totally taken over! Tears streaked down Pascal's cheeks, his mother was holding him tight and tried to console him.

But then they both saw Simon stir. He was not dead after all! He opened his eyes, but found it hard to focus. He tried to prop himself up on his elbows but crashed back onto the floor. Pascal could not gauge whether this was because Simon was still drunk or because he had seriously injured his father.

"I have to call an ambulance", Nathalie said in as calm a voice as possible. She untied herself from her son's tight embrace and ran down the hall towards the telephone.

Pascal could still not believe what had just happened. He had just wanted to use his mind-

sucking to stop his father from beating him up. And now Simon appeared to be severely injured, possibly incapacitated for life. Sitting up in bed, Pascal sobbed loudly. This time he knew that his life would never be the same again.

14

20 to 16 years ago

After the rape and murder of Markus, the shy and lonely German boy, Kevin's life was in turmoil. Although a strange feeling of elation continued for months after the rape, after a few months the weight that had initially been taken off Kevin's shoulders reared its ugly head again. He still did not feel bad about having taken somebody's life. That was not the problem. The problem was that he realised how lucky he had been with Markus. By chance or coincidence he had picked a boy who was a stranger in other kids' eyes, a loner who was easy to persuade to follow him wherever he wanted. And he had been lucky that it had all worked out on the moor, although his rape and murder had been so unplanned. In other words, even at the immature age of 14 Kevin realised that he had 'got away with murder' and that it would be very difficult to replicate what he had done to and with Markus with another boy in the near future.

What was most astonishing, however, was how little attention Markus' disappearance got at school. To be sure, there was some chatter about 'a boy from 1st grade disappearing' among Kevin's

schoolmates, and for a few days it was a discussion topic amongst the kids on the school yard, but, after all, hardly anyone had known the German boy and nobody knew what had happened to him. Markus was described almost like a ghost or a shadow at school whose presence was only acknowledged after he had disappeared. Most assumed anyway that the 'German weirdo' had just run away, possibly to go back to Germany, although rumour had it that Markus' father still worked in Harbourtown. In other words, nobody really cared, a fact further exacerbated by the complete lack of reporting of the case in the local and regional media. As far as Kevin could remember, the police had also not turned up at their school as the case was still classed as a 'missing boy' case rather than a murder.

Although this all meant that Kevin *had* got away with murder this time, Kevin kept a very low profile at school, hoping that nobody had seen him lurking around Markus just before the boy's disappearance. But the fact that he did not want to approach other 11- or 12-year-olds, at least for the moment, meant that Kevin's sexual frustration began to gradually overwhelm him again. The only solace for Kevin was to replay the rape of Markus in his mind over and over again, even despite the fact that Markus' body had not responded in the way Kevin had imagined it would. Of course, Kevin had tried to masturbate again, but whatever he did, stroking his

penis immediately conjured up images in his mind of awful Keith lying on top of him, resulting in the fact that his penis would stay limp. While masturbating Kevin then tried to brush aside any thoughts of Keith by concentrating hard on every minute detail of his rape of Markus, when he'd had no problems at all getting an erection, and on his overwhelming orgasm when he had taken the German boy from behind. But none of these thoughts elicited the required response in Kevin's penis, which stubbornly stayed limp. It became evident that Kevin could only be aroused in the presence of another young boy, and the only unsatisfactory sexual release Kevin had was his sporadic and unpredictable wet dreams.

Kevin was a bright boy and, of course, he realised that his sex life was completely abnormal. While his schoolmates increasingly talked about their first sexual experiences with girls and their growing masturbating prowess, Kevin had nothing to report. He could not make himself come and the only way he could get sexual satisfaction would be by raping another young boy. Throughout his last years at school he was torn between scouting out new young preys either in the schoolyard, the centre of Harbourtown, or just when he walked along the streets back to the shabby and small two-bedroom terraced house close to the dockyards where he lived with his mum. Occasionally he would catch a

glimpse of a young boy he liked. On several occasions he had spent several days scouting out one specific boy, but never had he found an opportunity again to lure one of the boys away to have sex with him.

Twice, when his sexual urges had taken the better of him again, he had been close to his goal. On the first occasion a young boy of about 10 had been willing to come with him to the edge of the moor after being promised 'play' and 'adventure', but, just as they started walking on one of the moorland paths, a family who apparently knew the boy crossed their path and had asked in an accusing tone what the boy was doing with a much older boy on the moor. The young boy immediately felt guilty of having joined Kevin and had walked back with the family, who kept on casting threatening glances back towards Kevin until they disappeared out of sight with the young boy in tow. On the second occasion, when Kevin was 17-years-old, he had lured away a boy of about 12 from a group of rough kids playing in the city centre, but, although the boy willingly followed him and was quite keen on an 'adventure' with Kevin, they were so far away from the moor that Kevin lost his way in the maze of Harbourtown suburbs and never found a spot where he could rape the boy without being seen.

The result of these misadventures increased Kevin's sexual frustration even more. As he grew

older and especially after his school had introduced psychology as an A-level subject, which Kevin found fascinating, at several points he began to wonder whether he should ask for professional psychological help with his 'condition'. He had by now realised that talking to his mother Sheryl would be absolutely hopeless. The whole episode with Keith had estranged them from each other for good, as Sheryl had never forgiven Kevin for Keith leaving. Even when Kevin was 18 years old and about to start studying geography at Harbourtown University, Sheryl still blamed Kevin for having 'lost Keith', especially because, after Keith, she never had a long-term relationship with a man again. On top of that, and although she had always drunk a lot, Sheryl had become a full-blown alcoholic. This meant that she had not only lost her job as a shop assistant and any prospects of meeting a sensible new man, but that she also was never in a fit state to hold a reasonable conversation with Kevin about anything. She did not even realise how well Kevin was doing at school, despite his miserable sex life and frustrations, and never acknowledged the fact that Kevin had had no problem being accepted into the Geography Department at Harbourtown University. In fact, Kevin's A-level results had been so good that he probably would have been accepted into most red brick universities in the UK.

But Kevin never mustered the courage to talk to a psycho-therapist or to seek professional psychological help. On the one hand, he did not want to admit to himself that he was 'nuts', especially as he outdid most of his schoolmates with his grades. In Kevin's eyes, most of his schoolmates, although most seemed to have healthy sex lives, were pretty weird and odd in other respects. So, to Kevin, he somehow did not think that he was weirder than others. On the other hand, and probably the key reason for not seeking psychological help, was the fact that Kevin did not want a shrink to dig deep into his mind to uncover the facts about Markus' rape and murder. Although Kevin was relatively confident that he could control his thoughts and emotions well, even in front of a stranger, what he had read about psychology for his A-levels suggested that some psychiatrists were very adept at bypassing one's protective emotional and psychological barriers. Kevin knew that he could not risk that. So he did not seek professional help, retreated back into his shell, stayed out of trouble at school, swallowed his dreadful loneliness and sexual frustration, and just got on with life. By the time he had started studying Geography at Harbourtown University, he had become so good at denying that he had a 'problem' that he almost felt happy for the first time in his life. And he greatly enjoyed studying Geography, as it allowed him to

delve deeper into his favourite subject of the resilience of vulnerable communities. He even began thinking about an academic career.

And then he went on his first Geography field trip to Brittany when his life changed again …

15

The present

Like the previous three days, Rachel and Inzuman were pouring over police files related to missing boys around Harbourtown over the past 40 years. The work was frustrating and slow and Rachel was tired. She leaned back in her creaking swivel chair – cuts in police resources meant that she had not been able to get a new office chair in years – placed her hands behind her head and yawned. Inzuman looked back at her with an understanding smile. He was also tired from the repetitive and, so far, unrewarding scrutiny of the police files.

Over the past week, Inzuman had made some progress on the 300 or so cases of local missing boys for the time period in question, and had by now managed to contact about 40% of the families of missing boys in the locality either by phone or in person. He had also been able to double-check the information relating to these 40% of cases with that provided in police files, which had allowed him to update some of these police files accordingly, especially if the missing boys had been found eventually. In one case, one of the missing boys had been eventually found 20 years after he had

disappeared. But, overall, the results had been frustrating. At least they now knew that all the 40% of boys whose families Inzuman had managed to contact could be excluded as possible victims, but this still left about 180 boys from the area who could be the possible moorboy victim. And, beyond this local Harbourtown sample, Inzuman had not even touched the files of the 2000 disappeared boys in the south-west of England, let alone beyond the south-west! Rachel and Inzuman, therefore, knew that they still had a huge task ahead of them, further hindered by the limited resources and manpower at their disposal. On top of this, they also had plenty of other cases they had to deal with, and Warrington was beginning to breathe down their necks urging them to show some results in the moorboy case.

In addition to all this frustration, Rachel had not slept well after coming back from the EIPT meeting in Paris. Despite Brian Bambridge's idiotic and bigoted comments, Rachel had greatly enjoyed the meeting and, especially, chatting to colleagues from all over Europe and hearing about their jobs and some of the key cases they were dealing with. Even after just one meeting Rachel also had a better understanding about the role that EIPT and *Interpol* played in trying to combat cross-border crime and how to better coordinate responses to it. She had enjoyed writing her report for the Home Office summarising the results of the first meeting, even if

this had meant coordinating what she wrote with that idiot Bambridge. But what Rachel had enjoyed most was meeting Stefan Scholz, the German representative at the EIPT meeting.

With a smile Rachel leaned back further in her swivel chair, and turned the chair a bit so that she could better look out of the window towards Harbourtown's western suburbs and the verdant hills of Cornwall in the distance. Although she had initially not intended to go to bed with any of her EIPT colleagues, especially not during the first meeting, the first night with Stefan had been very enjoyable. They had made love very gently and Rachel had been impressed at how careful and loving Stefan had been, asking her with every move and change of position whether 'it was alright' or whether 'it hurt in any way'. Rachel thought that she detected something about Stefan while they made love that suggested that either he had been deeply hurt, emotionally and physically, by another woman in the past, or, more worryingly, that he might have hurt another woman himself. Stefan had seemed almost over-cautious and hesitant and, at first, Rachel had to encourage him to be a bit more forceful, to penetrate her deeper and harder and, after trying out various variations of the missionary position, to take her from behind after which they both had come almost simultaneously. After their excellent meal out in Paris, Stefan had spent the

whole night with Rachel and they had made love again in the morning before breakfast, both of them hungry for each other's bodies and realising that this was the most rewarding love-making they both had had for a long time.

Stefan had ended up spending all three nights of the EIPT meeting at her hotel, and after three nights of love-making, banter, talking and laughing they had felt very comfortable together. They both realised that they were well suited for each other, although they both left the meeting without further promises or firm commitments to each other. Maybe that had been a mistake, and was one of the reasons why Rachel had not slept well these past few nights. She longed to ring or text Stefan, whose mobile number she had, but she was a bit reluctant to make the first move in what could become a long-term relationship. *Why am I so hesitant?*, Rachel wondered about herself. *I guess it's because I have been burnt by all these married lovers I've had in the past. But then, Stefan is divorced, so maybe ...*

The phone in front of Rachel rang and Rachel picked up the receiver, still half entranced by thoughts about Stefan's lovemaking.

"Hello Rachel, this is Hazel Molfese from the forensic lab", the Italian's voice was audible through the phone with the familiar accent Rachel liked. "I have further news regarding the analysis of moorboy's remains. Have you got a minute?"

Rachel uttered a "yes, good to hear from you" into the phone. She was glad for Hazel to have brought her back into the brutal reality of her job. The frustration of lack of progress in moorboy's case nagged at her.

"You won't believe it", Hazel continued, "but we have identified a second set of DNA among the boy's remains. My conclusions about what this could mean for the case are not very pleasant, so you better sit down …"

Now Rachel's senses were on full alert. This sounded both disturbing and interesting.

"As we've already discussed, DNA can be preserved in moorland bodies thanks to the anaerobic conditions that prevail. But, as we saw when you were last at the lab, moorboy's body had been disturbed, either by animals or by erosive processes, which is why extracting the DNA from the boy himself had not been easy, and why hardly any of his clothing survived."

Rachel remembered that only a fragment of the boy's t-shirt had survived and that there had been no evidence of other clothing such as a school uniform, which could have made identification so much easier.

"We assume that, if other clothing had been near the body, it completely rotted away over the years", Hazel continued, "especially if the clothing was situated to the body's right side which was more

severely affected by erosion and exposure to the elements, while the bit of t-shirt that has survived intact was found under the body, in other words it had been protected by the boy's body and had remained more-or-less in anaerobic conditions."

Hazel waited a few seconds for this information to sink in before she continued. "Now, the same seems to have happened to the second set of DNA we discovered, and we are certain that this DNA is from somebody else. This set of DNA was discovered inside the peat we found in the boy's pelvis ... and the possible explanation of this is why I asked you to sit down."

Rachel could already guess at what Hazel was pointing at.

"Although we can't be one hundred percent sure about the provenance of the DNA, i.e. what specifically was the original fluid or other source of the DNA, we think that it might have been the murderer's sperm left inside the boy's anus ..."

Although she knew that this was the most likely explanation, Rachel still gasped at the sheer atrocity of what she was hearing. Inzuman glanced up from the pile of police reports and stared at Rachel with a worried look. Rachel had put the phone on speakerphone, and Inzuman had heard every bit of the conversation. Rachel nodded back to reassure him that she was alright.

"I guess you know what this means", Hazel continued with hesitation in her voice. "Moorboy was raped and then killed, and the murderer made no attempt at all at hiding his possible identity, for example by wearing a condom."

Rachel could not resist conjuring up in her mind the gruesome image of this poor frail young boy being brutally raped between bushes on Devonmoor, the sheer brutality and depravity of the act, the pain and fear the boy must have been feeling. *This makes me want to solve the case even more urgently!*, Rachel thought, clenching her fists in anger. *We will catch this bastard, even if the rape and murder date back 30 or so years!*

"Of course we have already sent the DNA sample for sequencing and have just had the result back. It is definitely male DNA, so that would confirm that it most likely would have been semen. We have already compared it with our existing database of known offenders for the whole of the UK", Hazel continued, pre-empting Rachel's next question, "but we've had no match so far."

Both women were quiet for a moment, letting the information sink in.

"This is both great and very sad news, Hazel, many thanks", Rachel broke the silence. "I guess, it is maybe not a surprise that this happened to that kid, considering where he was found and how he had been killed. Maybe that also explains why we

have found so little clothing. The boy was probably naked when he was dumped in his shallow grave and the murderer might have discarded the other bits of clothing elsewhere." Rachel paused a while and heard a faint acknowledgement from Hazel that this might be a good explanation for the missing clothes. "The next step will be to send the results of the DNA sequencing to our European colleagues to see whether we can get any matches there?", Rachel asked.

"Yes, that's the next step", Hazel confirmed, "although it may now take even longer than before to get results because of Brexit which has certainly not made UK-EU collaboration easier!"

This is precisely where organisation such as EIPT come in!, Rachel thought, for a brief instant conjuring up the image of Stefan's face and body in her mind again. But Rachel had to admit that she did not yet know much about how this international collaboration on DNA analysis worked and was quite happy to leave this for Hazel to sort out.

"OK, Hazel, that's great, many thanks again for the info. I leave all the DNA stuff in your capable hands and look forward to hearing about further results in due course. At least we know now that we are dealing with a murderer *and* rapist which might help us further with the psychological profiling of the murderer."

Rachel hung up the phone. In her last comment, Rachel had alluded to their recent attempt to draw up a psychological profile of moorboy's murderer with the help of a forensic psychologist. Although budgets were stretched, and although Superintendent Warrington had first to be persuaded that this was a worthy investment for a single case like this – normally psychological profiling was only used in the case of serial killers – Harbourtown Constabulary had finally agreed to devote some funds for the establishment of a psychological profile of moorboy's murderer. Although still a far shot, especially as they only had one victim dating back years ago, psychological profiling could, at times, greatly aid at whittling down the number of suspects to a handful of possible individuals. But, first of all, they still needed to identify who that poor boy was and then, hopefully, who his sadist murderer and rapist was.

Rachel leaned back again in her creaking swivel chair. She was unsure whether she could find energy to go back to the pile of police reports in front of her.

16

16 years ago

Kevin had sneaked out of their youth hostel after dinner. He was a few weeks into his Geography degree at Harbourtown University and was attending his first field trip in the town of Morlaix in Brittany, north-west France. About 120 students and ten academics were based at the Morlaix Youth Hostel, just ten minutes' walk from Morlaix city centre. This destination was an obvious one for the Geography Department at Harbourtown University as Brittany was easily accessible from Harbourtown by ferry across the English Channel.

As he walked towards the centre of Morlaix in the fading light, Kevin thought back about his first few weeks of study. He had no doubt that he had made the right decision to choose to study Geography. He enjoyed the course, especially the human geography side of things. He particularly enjoyed the lectures by Prof Wilkinson on the resilience of human communities which chimed perfectly with Kevin's long-standing interest in the topic. He quickly had realised that all the readings on the topic he had done as a kid and teenager paid off, as his basic knowledge about how human

communities were affected by different types of disturbances by far exceeded that of his fellow students, even with some coming from far better and 'posher' schools than himself.

But, overall, Kevin's status and standing among his Geography student peers was not dissimilar to the status he'd had at school: most of his fellow students saw him as a loner and as a bit of a weirdo. He tended not to mix with his fellow students, and he hated all the drinking, partying and girl-chasing that went on. His evident specialist knowledge of anything to do with resilience had also not greatly endeared him to his fellow students, who were much keener on drinking and having a good time then on studying and specialising in specific geography topics. To most of them, the latter would come largely in the third year when they had to think about their undergraduate dissertations.

It was precisely this drinking and having fun that his fellow students were pursuing on this second evening in the various pubs and nightclubs in Morlaix, and Kevin did not want any part of it. That was the reason he had sneaked out early and on his own, immediately after the evening meal at the youth hostel was finished. He glanced behind him in the hope that no band of raucous students was following him, but he could see nobody.

Kevin had a specific destination in mind. He was excited, partly because a plan had begun to

form in his head since his arrival in Morlaix. Kevin was, indeed, desperate. It had been over four years since he had raped and killed Markus, and at age 18 his sexual lust was nearing its biological peak. And yet he could still not find a way to find sexual release by himself, the psychological masturbating blockage that had marred his whole teenage life persisted unchanged. Although he had not made any plans before the trip to use the opportunity to satiate his sexual lust, in his mind he had begun to imagine that being in a different country like France might offer new opportunities that could be less risky than if he perpetrated another murder back home. Every year that passed after Markus' murder, Kevin had been relieved to see that Markus' body had not yet been found. But Kevin also realised that he had recklessly left his sperm inside Markus' body four years ago. He knew nothing about how well sperm survived over the years, especially in a moorland environment in which Markus' body rested, but he had also been well aware over the past four years that he could not leave another DNA trace in another victim back home. That was simply too risky.

But what about perpetrating the same type of crime in another country? Again, he knew nothing about how European countries collaborated – if they collaborated at all – over individual cases of murdered and raped kids, but he was pretty sure that

if these instances were kept in isolation, i.e. only one murder at most perpetrated by him in a given country, the suspicion of the police authorities that a serial killer was on the rampage would be minimal. How could the police force in Morlaix know that a similar murder had occurred just across the Channel four years ago? Of course, Kevin could use a condom when raping another boy, but, considering his sexual problems and the inability to masturbate, he was convinced that the pleasure he had felt when he had raped Markus was only achievable without a condom. Committing a rape in another country could, therefore, allow him to remain reckless when it came to leaving his DNA inside the body of his victims.

As he walked through the town centre of Morlaix, the thought alone about future victims gave Kevin an erection. He adjusted his stiff penis through the lose trousers he was wearing so that it was not too evident to passers-by.

But although Kevin had contemplated the possibility of using the Geography field trip to Morlaix as a venue for his next rape, he could not know in advance whether an opportunity would arise. How could he scout out a boy if he was part of a group of students doing a project? Would he find an opportunity to be on his own for hours? And he knew nothing about the locality, so how would he find a good spot to find a victim? At the

beginning of the fieldtrip his plans for a rape were, therefore, very hypothetical. But then by luck he had found an opportunity on the very first day of the fieldtrip. Partly linked to his pet subject of resilience, Kevin had chosen the topic of 'the geography of poverty in Morlaix' as his student project for the fieldtrip. All students had to choose a project, and assessment for the fieldtrip was based on writing a report about the findings of their projects. While these projects were jointly undertaken by groups of six to eight students, who had to think about a common methodology how to assess their project's questions, luckily for Kevin they had to go out and collect data individually. In the case of Kevin and his group, this consisted largely of a mapping exercise to assess where pockets of deprivation could be found in Morlaix, and to analyse in their report why poorer districts were located in specific parts of the town. Coincidentally, this had given Kevin the opportunity from the very first day to scout out the most run-down neighbourhoods located towards the eastern side of Morlaix, away from the wealthy areas near the estuary and marina and town centre.

It was at this point that the plan had begun to emerge in Kevin's mind that he could use this fieldtrip for his depraved sexual needs. So, on the first day, he had already been on his own for hours, scouting out decrepit housing estates, and then

reporting back about his findings to his project group late afternoon. Kevin had to draw maps of the estates and their location for his project, but Kevin's main aim was to identify areas where young boys could be found, to find appropriate hiding places, and, most importantly, to find an area he could return to and rape a boy without being spotted. After a few hours on the first day, he had found the ideal spot: a run-down housing estate in the east of Morlaix, plenty of unattended kids running around, and a set of grubby garages behind which he could hide and observe the kids playing. Kevin spent about one hour, glued to the same spot behind a garage, and observing kids being beaten up by older kids, some youngsters evidently selling drugs to other kids, and some older kids injecting what was probably heroin. Most importantly, Kevin had spotted a beautiful young boy, probably about 11-years-old, slim and slender, with the dark-haired and white-skinned Celtic look prominent among many local Brittany residents.

It was to this spot that Kevin had returned after the evening meal on the second day. Of course, he did not have a clue whether he would see the Celtic-looking boy again, whether the boy's parents would allow him to be out in the street after dark, and whether his plan to assault the kid would work at all. As he approached the area he had scouted out the day before, Kevin was, therefore, very nervous.

He positioned himself behind the garage he had found the day before, and looked out towards the estate. It was about 7pm and most French families were eating dinner, so only a few people could be seen walking around. A group of kids played nearby and shouted to each other in French. It was a group of boys and they were having an argument over a football which one boy was holding and the others tried to snatch off him. Kevin was pleased to see that the boy holding the football was the 11-year-old Celtic-looking boy he had spotted the day before. The three other boys, older and much stronger, ganged up together and managed to tear off the football from Celtic boy's embrace, with one of the older boys pushing Celtic boy hard to the ground. While Celtic boy was lying there in the mud, the three other boys pounced on him and kicked him hard. Celtic boy tried to protect his face and chest with his hands and arms, but there was not much he could do. The other boys kicked him hard, causing Celtic boy evident pain. After a while, the other boys finally let go and walked away with the football, laughing and shouting obscene remarks back at Celtic boy who lay on the ground in a foetal position and hugged himself while sobbing loudly.

Watching this scene unfold, Kevin had to hold himself back not to go to the rescue of the boy while he was being beaten up. But his common sense prevailed. Under no circumstances could he allow

himself to be seen by the other boys. His whole plan was based on the fact that nobody other than the victim should see his face.

After a minute or so, the other boys had disappeared, but Celtic boy was still lying whimpering in the mud. Kevin glanced around him to see whether anyone else was approaching, but nobody could be seen in the dark and poorly lit carparks and garage forecourts. Kevin mustered all courage he had and walked towards Celtic boy. The boy shook with fear and blood ran down from a deep gash over his left eyebrow. The other boys had beaten him up pretty badly! Kevin grabbed one of the boy's arms and helped him to stand up. Celtic boy was unsteady on his feet and Kevin had to support him, nudging him slowly towards the row of garages. Celtic boy was so dazed from the beating that he let the stranger guide him by the arm. The boy was still snivelling and wiped his snotty nose with the back his hand. It was only then that he looked up at Kevin for the first time and realised that he did not know the young man who was dragging him towards the back of the garages by the arm. He tried to wrench himself from Kevin's grip, but Kevin held him very tightly now, dragging the boy's slim frame towards the spot behind the garages. At 18, Kevin was not very tall and muscly, but he still towered over Celtic boy and had no

problems pulling the boy behind him, all the while making sure that nobody was watching them.

Celtic boy had now fully come out of his beaten-up-stupor and began to shout and flay his arms and legs wildly about him. He wanted to run away. But Kevin had a firm grip around the boy's slender neck and a hand on his mouth. Only muffled sounds were audible from the boy's mouth. Kevin had now reached the spot behind the garage where he knew they could not be seen from the estate, and garages on the other side hid the view from anyone on the road. Kevin was now very aroused. He could not believe how lucky he had been that Celtic boy had been out and about at this time of day and that the other boys had basically done the job for him by beating up the boy badly, leaving the boy dazed and confused and relatively helpless. He certainly would have found it much more difficult to drag the struggling boy across the open expanse in front of the garages had Celtic boy been fully alert.

Kevin now entered a state of complete sexual frenzy, a state where he no longer recognised himself. Kevin's body totally took over from his mind, and it seemed to Kevin as if he had done in his mind what happened next a thousand times before. It was as if every movement had been practiced over-and-over in his depraved imagination. First he yanked the boy's jogging trousers down. They were fairly loose and easy to

pull down. Then he pulled down the boy's underpants and grabbed the boy's penis in his left hand. Although the light was poor and it was now almost pitch black, Kevin could not stop himself staring at the boy's hairless penis in the dim light emanating from a nearby streetlight. The boy was beautiful and Kevin was so turned on that he almost had an orgasm there and then. Kevin closed his eyes for a brief moment, held the boy tighter, and let the feeling of his onrushing orgasm ebb away. He certainly did not want to spoil the fun by coming too early! He pulled the boy's trousers and underpants over the boy's feet and managed to yank the boy's t-shirt off, pulling hard on the boy's arms while doing so. For a brief moment, Kevin had to use both his hands to pull the t-shirt over the boy's head, and Celtic boy immediately started shouting. Luckily for Kevin, the boy's sobs drowned out his yell, and Kevin was pretty sure that it had not been audible beyond the garages. He immediately put his right hand back on the boy's mouth and applied more pressure on the boy's neck, nearly strangling him. The boy let out choking sounds and fought for breath.

Kevin loosened his own belt, opened the zip of his trousers and let his trousers and underpants fall down to the muddy ground. He was pleased about his choice of clothing which allowed quick and easy opening and undoing. Kevin felt Celtic boy's naked

bottom against his stiff penis. Although Celtic boy was struggling as hard as he could, Kevin wanted to extend this feeling of utter pleasure for as long as possible. The rape of Markus, which he had played over-and-over in his mind over the past four years could now be supplemented by these exquisite memories of Celtic boy's rape. Kevin knew that he had to savour every second of this, as in a moment it would all be over.

With his left hand, Kevin searched for the boy's anus. As Celtic boy realised what was going to happen he increased the effort of trying to free himself from Kevin's brutal grip. But Celtic boy was not strong enough against an almost fully-grown adult. Kevin inserted his left index finger into the boys anus and felt the sphincter muscle tighten around it.

"Relax, or I'll kill you!", he hissed in English into the boy's ear. "Relax! Do you hear me!"

Celtic boy was whimpering in Kevin's stranglehold. Although his English was rudimentary, he understood the word 'relax' as it was almost identical with the French word 'relaxer'. He had realised by now that any resistance was futile and he understood what the man wanted from him. Maybe the man would let him go if he let him do with him what he wanted? With Kevin's finger still hurting him inside his anus, the boy tried to relax. After a few seconds, Kevin could feel the

boy's sphincter muscle's stranglehold around his finger relax a little and then the pressure abated completely. Kevin could now move his finger in and out of the boy's anus with relative ease. Kevin took his finger out and carefully pushed his stiff penis towards the boy's anus. This was the crucial moment, Kevin knew, as if he could not penetrate the boy properly all this would have been futile. But to Kevin's immense relief he managed to insert his penis into Celtic boy's anus without too much resistance. He knew that he was hurting the boy as Celtic boy's body stiffened under Kevin's stranglehold with every push deeper into the boy. Kevin had now almost fully inserted his penis inside the boy and felt a level of arousal he had not felt since raping Markus. But with Markus he had come almost immediately, now he wanted to extend this pre-orgiastic feeling for as long as possible. Fully inside Celtic boy's anus now, Kevin at first did not move at all. He just wanted the feeling of the boy's warm, moist and tight anus around his penis, smell the boy's hair under his chin, feel the boy's smooth and white skin under his stranglehold. His left hand found the boy's limp penis and started stroking it, pushing the boy's foreskin gently back and forth. At this point Kevin did not want to hurt the boy. He wanted the boy to feel as much pleasure as he did, as much pleasure as he had felt when bastard Keith

I'm not able to help with this.

when his violent orgasm had abated did he try to stifle his groans.

While still inside the boy, he pulled Celtic boy tightly towards him in an intimate embrace that almost suggested tenderness and caring. Celtic boy had his eyes closed and just waited for what would happen next, like a scared rabbit caught in the full-beam headlights of an oncoming car. But Kevin, despite the momentary tenderness, and possibly even love he felt for the boy at that very moment, knew that he now had to do the inevitable. His mind had switched back on from his frenzied and uncontrolled state. Kevin pulled out his now limp penis from the boy's anus. He could feel the boy wriggling in his stranglehold. *I have to do it! I have to do it!*, Kevin shouted inwardly at himself. There was hesitation, there were some remnants of humanity within Kevin at this moment in time, there was some compassion towards the boy who had given him so much pleasure. But Kevin knew that, as with Markus, he could not let the boy live. Without much further thinking about the situation, Kevin tightened his stranglehold around the boy's neck. The boy now struggled again hard to wrench off Kevin's tight grip with both his tiny hands, but Kevin only strengthened his hold. After about ten seconds Celtic boy stopped struggling and his body fell limply into Kevin's arms. Kevin applied his

stranglehold for another ten seconds and then let the dead body of the boy slump to the muddy ground.

Kevin quickly pulled up his trousers and underpants and was relieved to see that they were not too muddy. He stood there for a while and stared at Celtic boy's frail and pale body lying on the ground. How small and vulnerable the boy looked! But Kevin did not allow himself to feel sad about the situation. He had to make sure now that he would escape without being seen. First, he listened out for anyone approaching, but all was quiet. He then carefully made his way towards the row of garages that had shielded them from the road and carefully peeked around the corner. There were some people in the far distance, and a car was just leaving the garage forecourt, but other than that all was calm. People were in their flats in the estate eating dinner. It probably would take a while for Celtic boy's body to be found.

Kevin made his way quickly through the estate, and walked back to the youth hostel via the town centre. Nobody seemed to pay any attention to him. Back in his room, he was alone as his fellow students were still out drinking in the town centre. Kevin knew from the night before that they would probably be so drunk that they would not remember much about the evening, let alone whether Kevin was in or not when they came back. He was safe from that side.

But doubts kept creeping into Kevin's mind. His attack on the boy had been so unplanned that he had not thought much about the aftermath of his actions. Maybe he should have waited another day? But then the same opportunity might not have offered itself? But they still had two days fieldwork in Morlaix. What if the police found the body soon and started an inquiry while he was still in Morlaix? It was unlikely that their investigation would include a group of British students on visit to Morlaix, and by the time they would possibly consider them they would be long back in Britain. But, lying in bed and playing through his mind the exquisite moments he had just felt with Celtic boy, Kevin was nonetheless worried about what he had just done. It had not been perfectly planned, and although he had been very lucky with how events had unfolded, the timing had not been great. He liked that fact that he had perpetrated his rape in another country and jurisdiction and that he would be long gone when the police investigation would really start, but it would have been better to commit the rape just hours before he left the country. He needed to take this into account for his next rape. With a smile, and feeling a bit more relaxed, Kevin closed his eyes.

17

The present

Pascal was desperate. It was raining hard and he was completely drenched. He had to find shelter soon or he would die of exposure. He hastened his steps and tried another door of the empty factory. To his surprise, the door opened with a rusty creak. Pascal stepped inside and turned on his torch. He was glad that he had remembered to pack a torch when he had hurriedly fled from home. And that he had also taken with him a sleeping bag, a few clothes, and some items of food that were in his backpack. But would it all still be dry?

The door opened onto a large hall full of rusty old machines, cables dangling down from the ceiling, and water dripping from leaks in the corrugated iron roof. It was difficult to make out specific details in the dark, but the place looked like it had been abandoned for years. Pascal walked to a patch of ground that seemed a bit drier, opened his pack and was relieved to see that everything inside was dry. He unfurled the sleeping bag and sat down on it, the beam of his torch only partly lighting the huge and spooky arena around him. At least he was dry. He grabbed a chocolate bar from his pack and

began eating it, realising that he was very hungry. After all, it had been over six hours since he had last eaten.

Pascal lay back on the sleeping bag and played through the events of last night in his mind: his dad Simon half-dead on the floor after Pascal's uncontrolled mind-sucking; his mum Nathalie frantically running around, panicked and on the verge of a nervous breakdown, and calling the emergency services; the ambulance finally arriving and taking his father away; Nathalie sobbing and staring at him with the inscrutable strange look on her face he had seen so often before. Although it had been the middle of the night, Pascal had not gone back to sleep. First of all, he was much too agitated after what he had done to his dad to be able to sleep, but, secondly, he did not want to be at home when the police arrived to question him about what had happened. After all, he had nearly killed his father, possibly incapacitating him for life! After waiting a while and listening out for Nathalie who had cried a long time but eventually must have gone to sleep in the bedroom next door, Pascal had cautiously got up, put on his clothes, grabbed his pack, stuffed his sleeping bag, some clothes and food from the kitchen into it, and had made his way out of their flat on tiptoes. He was unsure whether he would see his mum ever again.

And now here he was: still in the suburb of Branlieu, as he had not walked very far from their housing estate, drenched, hungry and tired. Had he done the right thing, running away? But Pascal was a smart boy. As soon as the ambulance had taken away his dad, he knew that his life would never be the same again. You could not continue as normal after nearly killing your dad! Pascal knew that there would be a police investigation, that he probably would be taken to some kind of institution and locked up there for years, probably one that was full of weird kids like himself. Nathalie would probably not even care too much if he was gone. Although she kind of loved him and did the odd nice things with him when Simon was not around, he had never received much support from his mum, certainly not about his special 'gift'. His mum saw him as a weirdo and was probably happy that he was finally gone!

But where could he go without being found by the police? Pascal was not a very street-wise kid and he did not even know his own neighbourhood of Branlieu well. But he had walked past this derelict factory building a few times before and had immediately thought about it as a place of refuge. At least for the moment. Until he had thought through a bit more about what he would do next.

Pascal lay down on the sleeping bag and closed his eyes. Tears began streaking down his cheeks and

he sobbed quietly. He knew that the next few days and weeks would be very hard.

18

12 to 10 years ago

The Brittany fieldtrip and the successful and highly pleasurable rape of Celtic boy had completely changed Kevin's outlook on life. He now knew what he wanted and needed: he had to find a job that would allow him to regularly visit various European destinations, ideally deprived urban housing estates where he could find innumerable possible victims, and ideally situated near airports for quick get-aways. And he also knew that he had to be patient, very patient, and that it could be years again before he could commit the next rape. But at least he now had two exquisite memories of boys' rapes: Markus, whose rape Kevin's acute mind still remembered as if it had happened yesterday, and Celtic boy where every microsecond of the act of rape remained deeply etched in Kevin's memory. Although he knew that his sexual frustration and lust would gradually build up again over the next few months, and probably even years, Kevin knew that he could live off these two memories for the time being. Until the next opportunity offered itself.

Kevin's plan was, therefore, to do a PhD in Geography after his undergraduate studies. He

would stay at Harbourtown University and choose Prof Wilkinson, the expert on resilience, as his supervisor. This plan further spurred on Kevin to do well with his studies, as only students with good upper-second or first-class degrees would be allowed into Harbourtown University's prestigious PhD programme. Unsurprisingly, and with few other distractions such as drinking and chasing girls, which often destroyed the academic aspirations of his fellow students, Kevin found it easy to concentrate on his university work, and he completed his degree after three years of study with a first-class degree, the third best result in his year's cohort. After this, his application for PhD study with Prof Wilkinson was only a formality and Kevin also successfully obtained one of the PhD grants offered by Harbourtown University, which, in turn, guaranteed his financial independence and would also pay for all his travels, subsistence and accommodation in his European case study sites.

Kevin had moved away from his awful mum Sheryl as soon as he had started university. But, by that time, Sheryl had already been so consumed by her alcohol addiction that she was barely able to live on her own anymore. Soon after Kevin had moved out she had been referred by social services to a residential alcohol rehabilitation centre in the centre of Harbourtown, where she would probably have to stay for years. Kevin had basically lost all touch

with Sheryl after this and, after a few unsatisfactory early attempts at seeing her at the rehab centre, had stopped visiting her altogether.

With his PhD grant, he was able to afford modest accommodation in a single bedroom flat with kitchen near Harbourtown's ferry terminal. He was particularly happy about not having to share a flat anymore with anyone else, which he had found particularly difficult during his undergraduate years with flatmates in shared university accommodation. And he had waited, patiently, not letting his sexual lust overwhelm him, like a hibernating animal in the deepest recesses of a cave. And that was probably how his university flatmates had largely perceived him: like a hibernating ghost, only half present, a shadowy figure in the background they could never fully understand, somebody utterly boring and uninteresting who did not share their primitive predilections for booze and fucking girls, in other words, he was seen as a complete loser, a weirdo and nutter that everybody tried to avoid. And this has suited Kevin perfectly: his flatmates had left him alone and he had left them alone, in his parallel universe of sexual depravity, in his small weird world of memories about the two rapes he had committed that got him through most of the days and nights. During his undergraduate years, his flatmates had often surprised Kevin sitting alone among the mess in their kitchen, smiling, not even

realising that they had come in, and thinking ahead about the time when he could rape again, when he could possess another boy, where he would be in full control again over this dreadful lust eating away at him every waking moment.

Kevin had chosen his PhD topic largely for tactical reasons to provide him with opportunities to find and rape young boys, although, he was not ashamed to admit to himself, that he was also interested in the topic from a research perspective. His research would be a comparative study across several European cities of the resilience of vulnerable deprived urban communities, a topic Prof Wilkinson found utterly interesting and which he supported enthusiastically. Kevin's plan was to rape a boy at every location and ideally near an airport for a quick get-away. His long-term plan was to avoid raping and killing in the same country more than once, to choose as many different countries as possible, and to never choose his victims in the same city twice so that police forces could never connect the dots, tie together the breadcrumbs he left, especially in the form of his DNA left inside the boys. If his rapes and murders were spaced out over months and years, all in different countries, jurisdictions and locations, how could different police forces ever suspect that all these rapes and murders of young boys were committed by one and the same person?

He shaped his research methodology accordingly, which would allow him to select many different European cities where he would spend only a short time in each. He knew that he had got away with bad planning in Brittany, and although he had seen the headlines in the local newspaper on the last day of the fieldtrip that the body of Celtic boy had been found the morning after his rape, Morlaix police, luckily, had never bothered the British Geography students at the youth hostel. But future rapes had to be timed much better. As a result, his rapes would always occur on the last day of his case study visits, just hours before boarding the plane in order to get out of the country before his victims were found.

The result of Kevin's meticulous plan was a dreadful rape and killing spree in various European locations during the three years of his PhD. His first case study, about 10 months into his PhD, was in Madrid where he successfully scouted out, raped and killed a ten-year old immigrant boy. The next rape and murder occurred just a few months later in Bordeaux in the south-west of France, where he had managed to lure a 12-year old boy into dense bushes of a small park located in Bordeaux's poorest neighbourhood. Although the boy had not been his first choice and was already a bit too old and tall, after a brief struggle Kevin had nonetheless managed to wrestle the boy to the ground, yank off

his clothes and rape him while lying on the ground. 16 months into his PhD he raped and killed a beautiful blond 11-year old boy in Munich, and three months later a very small boy, who might have only been 9-years-old, in Prague. With the latter, Kevin's aggressive penetration of the boy's anus had severely injured the boy and Kevin suspected that the boy would have died of blood loss anyway had it not been for the rapid strangling after the act. Because it had been such a bloody affair, Kevin had not enjoyed the act so much, and he swore to himself that in future he would only choose boys that were a bit older and more mature. 11-year-olds were perfect in that respect and Kevin still hoped that, at that age, he might even one day elicit a sexual response from one of the boys. So far, they had all been too scared and in too much agony to show any sexual response, and the 9-year-old in particular could not be expected to show much sexual response at that age.

But that not everything could go according to plan became particularly evident in the third and final year of Kevin's PhD. Although he had one very successful and highly memorable experience with a skinny 11-year-old immigrant boy in Amsterdam whose lack of struggle had allowed Kevin to prolong the rape and pleasure beyond anything he had experienced before, two botched attempts in Gent, Belgium, and in Luxemburg had

immensely frustrated Kevin. Although he had successfully scouted out a boy in the most deprived neighbourhood in Gent for two days in a row, on the third day, just before his flight back to the UK, the boy was nowhere to be found, and no quick replacement was evident. This had meant a flight back without release of Kevin's pent-up sexual lust. In Luxemburg, Kevin's experience was even worse. In his original plan to select Luxemburg as a case study city, Kevin had underestimated both how small this European capital city actually was and how close-knit a community it was. As one of the wealthiest cities in Europe, indeed in the world, Luxemburg did not have many deprived neighbourhoods, and in the two areas Kevin eventually selected as possible sites for his next rape, all the kids seemed to be well protected by adults and were rarely out playing on their own, especially after dark. Although Kevin had spotted a boy, probably about 10- or 11-years old, whose appearance he particularly liked, he never even came close to the boy, let alone to be in a situation where he could successfully snatch the boy away.

After these two botched attempts, Kevin had come back to the UK utterly frustrated and less sure about his future plans. It was at this time that he thought about possibly filming his next rape, so that he could draw on real pictures to remind him of his rape rather than having to rely on his memory, just

in case if planned future attacks were not successful. Kevin had to admit that although he still vividly remembered all the seven rapes he had so far committed, they began to blur into one and he found it increasingly difficult for his mind to disentangle individual memories. But he was also wary of the idea of filming already then, as the danger to be found with evidence on him about his dreadful deeds was simply too large.

Still his bedtime routine was always the same, with or without filmed evidence: after reading a bit, he would switch off the light and ease himself to sleep by thinking about one of his seven rapes so far, trying to play through in his mind every exquisite second of the rape and trying to remember the associated feelings, smells, sounds and noises. His thoughts then focused specifically on the seconds before his orgasm, the exquisite arousal of pent-up lust and energy and the eventual release inside the boys. But these thoughts never gave him an erection, his penis stayed limp, like a dead nerveless wooden stick. Only through physical interaction with boys, through the act of rape, did it appear that any life could be injected into the useless appendage between his legs. But although these memories never arose him, they always quickly sent him to sleep.

The time after his two botched rape attempts was a tough one was Kevin. Not only was his sexual

frustration at its peak, as he had not found sexual release for many months, but he also was stressed by writing up his PhD and by applying for jobs. But, despite his recent setback, Kevin was by now convinced that the life of an academic was the perfect disguise for his depraved sexual needs. As an academic he would be free to choose what research he wanted to do and where, he would have access to research funds that would considerably lessen the financial pressure to pay for expensive flights and accommodation in his European locations, and he would have plenty of time and good excuses to scout out young victims as part of his 'field work'. No other job would offer him such opportunities.

As luck had it, a lecturer post in Geography was advertised at Harbourtown University just when Kevin was completing his PhD. With strong support from his supervisor Prof Wilkinson, whose reference and opinion played a key role in the candidate selection process, Kevin got the job. He now was settled in Harbourtown with a permanent job, a good salary, and all the freedom in the world to satisfy his sexual lust. Now the only thing he had to hope for was that he would successfully scout out a prey at his next chosen location and be able to drag the boy to a safe spot to be raped and killed. Upon starting his new job, Kevin had immediately put in for a small British Academy research grant that

would pay for his next planned trip to study the resilience of deprived neighbourhoods. His next 'case study' would be in Brussels, Belgium.

19

The present

"Rachel, you better sit down!"

Rachel knew that something ominous was about to be revealed upon hearing these words. Last time it had been when Hazel divulged that moorboy had not only been brutally murdered but also raped. This time it was Stefan Scholz at the end of the line with what was undoubtedly unexpected news.

"The two DNA samples match!", Stefan shouted into the phone, unable to hide his excitement. "When I first saw the result I could not believe it!"

Rachel was flabbergasted. It was indeed good that she had sat down as this news was unbelievable. She glanced around her cosy kitchen, with the herbs on the wall and the sunlight warming up the room. She just could not believe what she was hearing.

"And you are sure that there is no mistake?", she asked incredulously. "That the samples haven been contaminated or something like that?"

"I thought exactly the same", Stefan replied. "But no. The forensic lab here has assured me that there was no contamination and that the result is genuine. The 30-year old DNA of your moorboy

murderer and that of our Nürnberg boy killer from 14 months ago are from one and the same person! It is unbelievable!"

Rachel had to take a deep breath and thought about how things had come to this. First of all, she had mustered up the courage to ring Stefan about a week after the EIPT meeting. Stefan seemed glad to hear her voice and claimed that he had been about to ring her himself. They had talked at length, first innocuously about the EIPT meeting, but very quickly their discussion had turned to the possible future of their 'relationship'. They both had evidently greatly enjoyed each other's company in Paris, the lovemaking, the laughing together, the nice meals, and they both agreed that they wanted more. For the first time in a long while, Rachel had felt completely at ease, not constantly doubting her decisions, as had been the case with her flings and affairs over the past few years. As she spoke to Stefan for the first time on the phone since the Paris meeting, a warm feeling around her tummy had manifested itself. She had felt good.

In fact, she had felt so good about the prospect of seeing Stefan again at the next EIPT meeting that she had immediately broken off with Gordon. Gordon had been his usual self, first not believing that it was Rachel who was breaking up their 'relationship' and not him, second begging Rachel to stay with him with the promise Rachel had heard

so often that Gordon would leave his wife and move in with Rachel. Rachel was glad when she found the courage to hang up the phone on Gordon and that she would never see him again. This chapter in her life was definitely over.

But that first phone call with Stefan after the Paris meeting had not only been about their budding relationship. Somehow their chatter had drifted towards the two boy murders they had both mentioned before and they had, almost jokingly, suggested to compare the DNA samples, as the cases, although decades apart, appeared to show some similarities. Although probably not allowed to do so based on the secrecy code linked to ongoing investigations, during this conversation by phone Stefan had specified further details about the murder of the 11-year-old boy in the district of Schönwalde in Nürnberg. Like moorboy, Jürgen Hänsler, as the boy was called, had been brutally raped and strangled. As with moorboy, the perpetrator had not made any attempt to prevent his semen from showing up in the analysis of the body. Like moorboy, Jürgen was a slim and rather small and pretty 11-year-old prepubescent boy. Like moorboy, Jürgen's body was found in a remote spot, on this occasion in bushes behind garages in one of the Nürnberg housing estates dating from the 1970s. But despite these parallels, neither Rachel nor

Stefan had thought that there could be a link between the two murders.

After this initial phone call with Stefan, Rachel had immediately contacted Hazel Molfese from the Harbourtown forensic lab and, to Rachel's relief, Hazel had been more than happy to immediately send the results of the DNA analysis of the semen left in moorboy to the forensic lab in Nürnberg. And now this unexpected result! The DNA between the two cases matched, and, according to the Nürnberg forensic lab, there was no doubt about the accuracy of the findings.

"But how can this be?", Rachel asked, placing her mobile back to her ear. "One murder here in Harbourtown about 20 years ago, the other in a medium-sized German city about one year ago? Does this not imply that there could be more such cases, maybe all across Europe?"

Rachel knew that she was clutching at straws as she had no evidence whatsoever for more such murders. "And, of course, you could also not find any DNA match with any of the samples in your data bank?", Rachel asked, just to make sure that she had not missed a vital clue.

"No, nothing", came Stefan's immediate reply. "Whoever that sick bastard is, he obviously has no police record in Germany. I also trailed the Europe-wide *Interpol*-based DNA data bank, i.e. beyond Germany, and also found nothing there. This

murderer and rapist of young boys has a clean slate and no previous convictions!"

"Look, why don't we raise this interesting result at the next EIPT meeting?", Rachel wondered. "As we already discussed over dinner at the Paris meeting, isn't this exactly what these meetings are for? I have seen in the agenda for the next meeting …", and Rachel searched in the pile of papers lying on the kitchen table in front of her, "… that they have scheduled a whole series of talks about … yes, here it is: about the most important crimes, or series of crimes, in committee member's respective jurisdictions, to see whether there are any international links between these cases. Wouldn't our discovery fit neatly into this?"

"Great idea", Stefan replied enthusiastically. "Let's do a presentation together where we present the key facts of our two murders and check whether any colleagues in other European countries have come across similar cases in recent times. I am getting really curious about this …"

After they had hung up, Rachel sat at her kitchen table for a long time. She still did not quite understand what was going on, but she looked forward to tell both Inzuman and Warrington about this. Finally some progress on this damn moorboy case, and from a rather unexpected corner!

20

The present

Rachel glanced at Stefan sitting next to her. They were in Rome, at the next EIPT meeting. Her gaze drifted towards the magnificent fresco on the ceiling of the grand room in the *Aurelius Palace* where the meeting took place. She could not stop herself feasting on the sight of the intricate 16th century painting by Salvatore Fontanelli depicting cherubs, angels and demi-gods ascending towards God towering on a shiny white cloud in the middle of the giant fresco directly above her head. Italian Renaissance art had always entranced Rachel, and now she had the privilege to sit right under one of Rome's most beautiful frescoes.

But Rachel's thoughts quickly drifted back towards Stefan and the night before. When she had first seen him again in the foyer of the *Hotel di Umbria* not far from the *Aurelius Palace*, she had felt like a little girl seeing her first crush again. These were feelings until recently unknown to her, especially on the back of her stupid affairs with all these half-committed married men. Stefan and her had kissed long and tenderly in the foyer, had gone briefly to the bar for a drink, but very quickly they

had then made their way to their shared room. They had made love tenderly, longingly and full of passion. She really felt comfortable and happy with this man, and it seemed to Rachel as if all her body was fully in tune with Stefan's body and mind. Could she at age 38 even envisage having children with him? Was it not too late already for her? And was it not too early to think of this after only two encounters?

But Rachel's attention quickly shifted to the next speaker who was addressing the audience of about 80 EIPT delegates. True to the agenda that had been circulated weeks ago, this first day of the meeting was dedicated solely to individual EIPT teams talking about current unresolved cases that might have international linkages, and whether the new burgeoning EIPT networks could possibly help in finding solutions to these cases. All morning, Rachel had been fascinated about the presentations that had ranged from a possible serial killer roaming European motorway service stations presented by the Swedish EIPT team; to a presentation by Swiss and Austrian EIPT members about a group of internet scam artists targeting old and single women and who probably operated in at least five European countries; to the current fascinating talk by the Polish, Czech and Hungarian EIPT teams about a ring trafficking Eastern European under-aged girls in nightclubs in at least six European countries. All

presenters had asked at the end of their talks for help from the delegates as to whether similar, but as yet not widely reported, cases had been identified in their own respective countries and whether further links to these reported cases were evident. Each talk had elicited an animated response from members of the audience, and in several cases anecdotal evidence about possible parallels to cases currently investigated in individual countries had already been provided, with promises made that further details would be made available over the next few days. As a result, there was already a real buzz about the meeting, and all EIPT committee members felt that they contributed something towards possibly solving cases with an international connection.

After a heated question-and-answer-session, the Polish, Czech and Hungarian teams had completed their presentation, and now it was Stefan's and Rachel's turn to talk about their two interlinked cases. As she walked up to the large podium in front of the room, Rachel caught sight of Brian Bambridge, her fellow British EIPT committee member, sitting on the other side of the room. Brian glanced at her with unhidden hostility, almost as if he accused her of betraying the British cause by giving a presentation with another European delegate. *What an asshole!*, Rachel could not prevent herself from thinking again as she refused to return Bambridge's solemn stare. *What a*

pompous pro-Brexit asshole! But Rachel had been relieved to hear from other EIPT members that a joke was already going around about Bambridge: when chatting to Bambridge everybody blamed everything that had gone wrong on their journey to Rome on Brexit. Missed at taxi, like the French EIPT representative had done? Blame it on Brexit! Missed a train in Spain? Blame it on Brexit? The coffee at breakfast lukewarm? Blame it on Brexit! It had taken Bambridge a while to realise that he had become the butt of collective jokes, and his reaction had been true to his despicable character: first a frown, then evident annoyance, and, finally, a loud snort and walking away from his offending colleagues. Bambridge was truly side-lined and he hated it! Luckily for Rachel, her evident anti-Bambridge stance from the beginning had shielded her from the evident anti-British undertone permeating EIPT meetings. And doing a talk with a highly respected German EIPT member had only raised her credentials among the other delegates.

It was, therefore, with head held high that Rachel stepped onto the podium with Stefan. This was not about Britain or Bambridge, this was all about trying to find out whether a serial killer of young boys had operated undetected in Europe for decades. Using *PowerPoint* slides, Stefan and Rachel presented the facts of their two seemingly unconnected cases: the similar age of the two boy

victims; that they had both been strangled; that they were of similar built and height; and, most importantly, that their murderer and rapist had left semen inside them whose DNA appeared to match. The delegates were baffled at hearing that it appeared that the same person had killed a boy in Harbourtown about 20 years ago and a boy in Nürnberg only 14 months ago.

When Stefan and Rachel had finished their presentation, a loud hum and murmur could be heard among the 80 delegates. Evidently their presentation had struck a chord and loud gasps had been evident when Rachel and Stefan had talked about the matching DNA. Committee members were talking to their neighbours, small groups were forming and exchanging information, and several hands went up indicating that people wanted to speak.

Rachel picked one of the raised hands at random and invited an elderly gentleman to speak. "Many thanks for your interesting talk", the man said with what was evidently a southern European accent. "I am one of the Greek EIPT committee members and your talk has reminded me of a similar case we had in Athens …", and he leaned over to his colleague on the right to seek confirmation, "…yes … we think it happened three years ago. I was not involved in the case myself, but I know a colleague from the *Eastern Athens Police Prefecture* who

mentioned an 11-year-old boy raped and strangled just the way you described it for your cases. I believe a leather belt was also used to kill the boy but I would need to check this ...", and he leaned over to his colleague again who frantically thumbed his mobile phone, "... ah yes ... a newspaper report from that time confirms that it was a leather belt, just like the one used in your case from Harbourtown. But we don't know whether any DNA was left at the scene, this I would need to check on my return after this meeting. No culprit has been found so far."

Rachel thanked the Greek delegate and was about to respond, but so many hands had gone up that she felt that others also needed to be allowed to speak as time was tight. She pointed at a woman sitting near the back row.

"Merci beaucoup for your stimulating presentation", the woman said with an evident French accent while standing up so that she could be better heard. "I am from the French EIPT group and, to the best of my knowledge and having just briefly spoken by phone to one of my colleagues in south-west France, we actually have two pending cases that more-or-less fit your case descriptions: one which dates a long while back in the Brittany town of Morlaix, possibly 15 years or so, I am not sure, and the other in the city of Bordeaux in south-west France which my colleague has confirmed was

12 years ago. Again in both cases the case description is similar, young boys aged 11 or 12, slim build, strangled and dumped naked probably where the rape happened, and with semen left inside the boys. I don't know at this stage whether a comparison of the DNA has ever been done … as Morlaix and Bordeaux are almost 700 km apart", she said glancing around slightly apologetically for what might have been an important omission by French police at the time, "but I will check immediately on my return. These cases are certainly still open and had independently generated considerable media attention at the time, but I am unsure whether they still are being actively investigated at this moment in time."

Many more hands were still up and Rachel and Stefan realised that they had opened a whole can of worms. Although they were running out of time as the next presentation had been due to start over ten minutes ago, the brief comments made by another four delegates revealed further similar cases in Madrid 12 years ago, Brussels about nine or ten years ago, Oslo six years ago, and Sarajevo just barely 12 months ago. Upon hearing the last comment from their Croatian colleague, and if these cases were indeed all connected, Rachel realised that the boy murderer might have killed a boy in Nürnberg and Sarajevo within the timespan of less than three months. This dreadful murderer was

clearly still out there, killing his young victims on a regular basis and within relatively short timespans.

Discussions were still continuing among the delegates and many more evidently wanted to have their say about similar cases, but with a glance at the chairman of the meeting, Dr Sonderegger from Switzerland, who had approached the podium pointing at his watch, Rachel and Stefan had to bring their session to a conclusion.

"OK, many thanks for all your comments and sorry that we do not have the time here and now to give all of you the opportunity to speak", Stefan said, stepping towards the front of the podium and asking the audience to quieten down. "But from the comments we have already received it appears that we *have* a serial killer of young boys at our hands who is acting with relative impunity across the whole of Europe. Although it is evident from what we have just heard from you that cases of murders and rape of young boys in your respective countries have been investigated in-depth and, in most cases, have elicited substantial national media responses, it is also evident that nobody has so far linked these various cases with each other. Of course, many of these cases might not be linked to our two cases where the DNA match confirms a connection. But, if it is one and the same murderer, it could well be that this is what this killer has been planning from the outset: to kill in different jurisdictions so that

national police forces would not be able to link individual cases together. In police jargon we refer to this as 'linkage blindness'. What I am saying is not meant to be a criticism of individual national police forces", and Stefan glanced apologetically towards Dr Sonderegger who nodded back encouragingly, "and occurs pretty much with all these cases we have heard this morning, whether it be serial killers or gangs trafficking young girls. But linkage blindness refers to the fact that it is difficult to establish common links between similar cases across different jurisdictions as, despite institutions like *Interpol* and now EIPT, we still tend to look at cases from a rather national perspective. And, as you all know as well as I do, although transnational European collaboration has improved over the past few decades, we are still far away from a truly pan-European police workforce that has access to all the data and information needed to solve such international cases. As you heard in our presentation, it was really only through sheer luck and coincidence that Rachel and I were able to link our two disparate cases together, but now it seems that we have opened a whole can of worms that might implicate almost all of you or your police jurisdictions in one way or another."

Stefan let his words sink in among the audience. He could see plenty of nods.

"The next step is pretty clear", Rachel picked up the thread and stepped forward towards Stefan at the front of the podium. "Based on your enthusiastic response already, could all of you please double-check with your national police jurisdictions whether you have similar cases that occurred in your respective countries and report back to me and Stefan. I think I am safe in assuming", and she quickly glanced over to Stefan, "that you are happy for me and Stefan to help with coordination of this effort of what we might term the 'European boy killer'. Of course, both Stefan and I need to take this higher up within our own police jurisdictions, and for me personally with the Home Office, as we are also working on other cases not linked to this investigation, but I assume that this will be allocated top priority if, indeed, all these boy murders are linked. So ...", and she glanced at the audience whose members nodded in acquiescence. Only Bambridge, sitting alone on the side, looked grumpily away. Rachel was evidently stealing all his thunder. "So, the next steps are clear. First, for those of you who have not yet told us about similar cases, let us know whether such cases have occurred in your respective countries. Please do this via e-mail or text us, or have a chat with us over the next few days. Second, if you can identify such cases, please send us the DNA results of the semen samples, if available, so that we can verify whether

all these murders have indeed been committed by one and the same person. Maybe we can then, at the next meeting ...", and Rachel glanced at Dr Sonderegger who nodded back again encouragingly, "present the preliminary findings and, for example, draw up a tentative timeline of the murders. Maybe we can then see whether there is a pattern emerging, and we can possibly even draw up a psychological profile of the murderer ..."

Rachel paused. She certainly had not expected the enthusiastic reaction they had received from their talk, and she had certainly not prepared anything she had just said in advance, nor had she coordinated this with Stefan beforehand. But Stefan's encouraging smile suggested to Rachel that she was saying the right things. She was grabbing the bull by the horns, she was taking the initiative. After all, this was exactly what these EIPT meetings should be about, and the continuing buzz among the audience confirmed to her yet again that they had touched a nerve. Her talk, but also the other talks earlier in the morning, had certainly given the EIPT a burst of energy and an excellent justification for why EIPT was important. Highly pleased with herself, and with appreciative nods form the audience, Rachel stepped off the podium. Bambridge made a point of looking away as she walked past him.

21

The present

Kevin was furious and had been in a terrible mood all afternoon. He was sitting in the plane on his return flight from Moscow, where he had attended a workshop on 'The resilience of communities affected by climate change'. Although the workshop was the last thing he wanted to think about, he had to admit that it had been interesting, especially the few talks he had attended, all held in English, by the Russian colleagues on Siberian communities affected by the melting of the permafrost.

But the workshop had, of course, just been another pretext to find a young boy to satisfy his warped sexual needs. As usual, he had planned his trip well: a country and a city he had never been to before to further blur the trail of rapes of murders he was leaving behind across Europe; the choice of a credible workshop which made it sound to his university colleagues back home in Harbourtown as if this was really the main reason for his trip; a workshop that had lasted four days which had given him plenty of opportunity to scout out decrepit Moscow housing estates for possible victims; and

wearing the right attire for his rape consisting of loosely fitting trousers that were easy to unzip and pull down while he held his victim in a stranglehold but that still appeared casual enough to make him look like an academic. And then the stupid boy he had so carefully chosen managed to escape!

Kevin gazed out of the plane window absent-mindedly and let the events of the past few hours go through his mind again. The landscape below was wintry, with patches of snow, barren forests, and small rural settlements huddled along meandering rivers.

And not only had this Moscow boy escaped, the first time this happened in well over 25 attacks on boys over the past 16 years or so, but this was now the second trip he had taken this year without being able to satiate his growing sexual lust! Just a few months earlier, on a trip to the Slovenian capital Ljubljana for a conference on the resilience of skiing resorts in the European Alps, he had failed to find a suitable boy, despite spending most of his time in the poorest parts of the city scouting out possible victims rather than attending the conference. This meant that he had now been without sex with a boy since his last successful attack in Albania's capital Tirana about 10 months ago.

Kevin closed his eyes and let this last rape play through his mind: in Tirana, one of the poorest cities

in Europe, he had found this beautiful-looking, wild and gypsy-like slim boy with long black hair, probably 11-years-old, and had raped him in the grounds of a derelict factory, after luring the boy with his usual promise of money. The boy had fought hard to escape and had even bitten Kevin in the right wrist – a visible injury Kevin subsequently had to hide from customs officials at Tirana Airport by holding a coat over his hand – but the boy's belligerence had increased Kevin's sexual arousal even more, and he'd had one of the longest, intensive and most powerful orgasms he could remember. But this had been so long ago, and, apart from his regular wet dreams, Kevin had not had any sexual release since.

Kevin clenched his fists in anger. Maybe he was losing his touch, or getting too old? Over the past seven years, if he recalled the timeline correctly, out of 18 planned attacks 6 had been botched, with the last two botched attempts this last year alone! In most cases he had just simply not been able to find a suitable boy, and he began to wonder whether the timeline he imposed on himself – for reasons of security and not to allow the police any time to identify him while he was still in the country raping and killing the boys just hours before boarding his return flight – was too tight and whether he needed to change his methodology. However, raping and killing boys with several days still left in the country

would exponentially increase the chances of getting caught.

But that he would let a boy escape had never happened before. Kevin closed his eyes and played through today's events in his mind again. He had identified a suitable boy three days ago in the infamous Moscow district of Somjenkowo, a district well known as a no-go area for visitors and reputed to be full of alcoholics and drug addicts. Even at daytime, Somjenkowo had indeed been a scary place, and Kevin had done his best to fit in by letting his shirt hang out, tousling his hair, and by just looking as dishevelled as possible. The result had been that nobody had bothered him in all the three days he had come to the area. On day two he had seen the same boy again, playing alone and looking bored, just the way Kevin liked it, and he had identified his usual favourite spot for the planned rape: a derelict area behind decrepit garages that was out of sight and not far from the playing field where the boy seemed to spend most of his time.

And the boy himself had been ideal: probably about 11-years-old, pre-pubescent, slim, tallish, blond, with a nice face with an aquiline nose, sharp features and deep blue eyes. And all had gone so well. He had successfully lured the boy to the back of the garages with a blue 1000-ruble banknote, about £10 or $13, which would have been a fortune

for a boy from this neighbourhood. Once he had reached the spot behind the garages he had, as usual, put one arm around the boy's neck and pulled the boy's trousers and underpants down and over the boy's grimy trainers. But then the zip of Kevin's own trousers somehow got caught in his underpants and for a brief moment, he had relaxed his grip around the boy's neck while tugging desperately to free his zip. In a flash, the boy had wriggled himself free of Kevin's stranglehold and had run away towards the playing fields, naked from the waist down. Kevin had been so stunned at the boy's quick reaction that it had taken him a few seconds to realise what had happened. He had quickly zipped up his trousers and left the area as quickly as he could. In the distance he could still hear the panicked boy shouting and alerting the whole neighbourhood. This was the first time ever, in Kevin's 20-year long raping and killing spree, that a boy had managed to escape! That a boy had seen his face! That a boy could identify him! And the boy would know that he was a stranger, as Kevin had spoken in English, not Russian, when he lured the boy away with his banknote.

To some extent this incident at least vindicates my methodology!, Kevin thought while glancing out of the window at the snowy landscape. They were probably somewhere above Belarus by now. *Although the boy probably quickly alerted*

everybody of what had happened, within two hours I was at Moscow's Sheremetyevo Airport, and within three hours on the plane! But Kevin recalled with trepidation the fear he had felt when arriving at the airport. As usual, he had first discarded the olive-oil-soaked rag he usually used to grease his penis before a rape, then he had retrieved his luggage from the locker where he had left it before going to Somjenkowo to rape the boy, and then he had briskly made his way to the check-in counter. But all the time he had glanced over his shoulder to see whether the police were already looking for him. But although he had seen plenty of armed police and soldiers, none of them had paid any attention to him. Only when he had successfully gone through passport control did Kevin's heartbeat slow down a bit, and once he was in the plane he had allowed himself to relax for the first time.

Now I am safe! I am safe!, he said to himself a few hours into the flight, trying to reassure himself. What could the boy and the Moscow authorities do? They would only have a vague description of some foreigner fondling a boy, nothing specific, nothing that could tie him to the attempted rape. And by the time the Moscow police got organised, if they got involved at all with a gypsy-looking kid, Kevin would long be back in Harbourtown, snug and safe in his flat near the ferry terminal.

Still, this was the first time he had to be afraid of the police of a country he had just visited, not a good omen for the future. He could never allow himself to let a boy escape again. If this happened too often, the police would eventually be able to stitch together a picture of him and could be on his trail soon. He had to be more careful! But on top of all this Kevin's sexual frustration was at its peak. Together with the time period about seven years ago, when he had tried Scandinavian destinations for his rapes and where he had two consecutive botched attempts in Helsinki and Stockholm, 10 months was the longest period without sexual release since Kevin had raped the boy in Morlaix on the Brittany Geography field trip 16 years ago. Sitting cramped in his airplane seat, Kevin could almost feel his swollen testicles pressing against his trousers. *And I still can't release myself!*, he thought while supressing a sob. He must have made a noise inadvertently as the passenger to his left – an obese lady with unhealthy skin and large rings on her fingers – stared at him inquisitively and with a frown before returning to her trashy magazine.

As a result of the Moscow debacle, Kevin already planned his next trip. Luckily, he still had plenty of research money on his university account, and there was a large resilience conference coming up soon. Although he had not intended to go abroad again that soon – normally a rape would 'keep him

going' and sexually satisfied for about 3-5 months – his need to find sexual release now forced him to use the next available opportunity. But, at the back of his mind, Kevin also knew that he was beginning to run out of new European destinations, unless he was willing to return to countries where had raped and killed before, which would, in turn, increase the risk of being caught. *Oh, it is all so fucked up!*, Kevin thought. *But this is another matter altogether, not something I want to think about now!* The prospect of raping another boy soon soothed Kevin's mind. With a smile on his face he gazed out of the window again. There was no need to panic. All would be well as usual. He had it all under control!

22

The present

"Many thanks for agreeing to be part of this EIPT sub-committee", Dr Sonderegger, the burly white-haired Swiss EIPT chairman, addressed the group of 30 EIPT members sitting in front of him. Among them were Rachel and Stefan who sat next to each other. They were at the next EIPT meeting held in Stuttgart, Germany, in a small side-room of the *Stuttgart Convention Centre* overlooking the Schlosspark, the gardens of the palace of the former kings of Württemberg, framed by old grandiose oaks and beech trees and interspersed with limestone-gravelled paths.

"As you know", Dr Sonderegger continued with his heavy Schwitzerdütsch accent, "the case of what we have termed for lack of a better alternative the 'European boy killer' has caused such a massive response and a stir among the EIPT and its parent organisations that we thought it wise to create this sub-committee dedicated entirely to shed more light on this dreadful set of cases. And I am very pleased that both the British Home Office as well as the Bavarian Innenministerium in charge of police affairs have agreed to grant special leave to both

Rachel Sontheimer from the Harbourtown Constabulary and to Stefan Scholz from the homicide division of the Nürnberg police force to devote all their time to this case", and he smiled gently at both Rachel and Stefan who acknowledged his kind words with a nod. "So, without further ado, I pass you over to Mrs Sontheimer and Mr Scholz."

Rachel and Stefan stood up and walked towards a screen situated at the top end of the room. Rachel was still not used of the European's rather stiff protocol of addressing her by her surname, and she had slightly flinched at Sonderegger's use of 'Mrs' when introducing her to the other colleagues in the room. But they had more important issues to discuss than inappropriately labelled honorifics.

As she walked towards the screen, the frantic last few weeks flashed up again briefly in Rachel's mind. The Home Office had been very supportive of her effort to bring the European boy killer issue to the attention of the EIPT, especially after her EIPT report had been highly praised, despite some futile attempts by the pompous idiot Bambridge to claim some credit for Rachel's story in the joint report. But her boss, Superintendent William Warrington, had been less keen. And Rachel did not blame him. Although the Home Office had promised additional funds for Harbourtown Constabulary to pay for a replacement for Rachel

while she spent most of her time on the European boy killer case, Warrington probably knew better than anyone that promises made by the Home Office were not always honoured. And where could they find a replacement for Rachel at such short notice and at a time when inspectors were leaving the police force in droves due to poor pay and poor work conditions? It was, therefore, with some trepidation that Rachel had accepted the EIPT offer to work full time on the boy killer case. To placate Warrington, she had agreed on a short-term period of absence of only three months initially, with the arrangement to be reviewed pending progress made at European level. And she had also promised to keep Sergeant Inzuman Patel and Superintendent Warrington informed of progress at all times.

Rachel stepped up to the screen and motioned to an assistant at the back of the room to turn on the *PowerPoint* beamer. A complex table with dates and names of places emerged on the screen.

"Hello everybody", Rachel said while clearing her throat. Although she had come well prepared, and although Stefan and her had meticulously gone through all the data they had been sent over the past three months by their European colleagues, she still felt nervous. Rachel knew that this was a big case and of possibly huge importance for many police forces around Europe.

"First of all many thanks to all of you and many of your colleagues both at EIPT and beyond who have sent us information about the possible European boy killer, based on Stefan's and my plea at the last EIPT meeting for coordinated data gathering on this case", Rachel said. "The response has, indeed, been enthusiastic and most information sent to us has been very detailed and helpful."

"And as you know", Stefan stepped in, "most of you have been asked to join this sub-committee as your countries are involved, in one way or another, in cases possibly linked to the boy killer."

"Indeed", Rachel confirmed while scanning the room. She recognised some faces familiar from the last meeting, including the Greek EIPT committee member who had mentioned a similar case in Athens, the French delegate who had mentioned the two similar cases in Morlaix, Brittany, and Bordeaux, south-west France, and the Spanish, Belgian, Norwegian and Croatian colleagues who had alluded to similar cases in their respective jurisdictions. "And here is the result of the information you all sent us", and she pointed at the *PowerPoint* slide on the screen. "As you can see, Stefan … Mr Scholz and I have summarised all this info into this table, which lists similar cases of young boys raped and strangled in the same way as our Harbourtown and Nurnberg cases mentioned in our initial talk at the last EIPT meeting."

The audience emitted an audible gasp as they saw the table showing the sheer number of cases.

"Now, it is unlikely that all these cases are linked to the same murderer, but, as we will explain shortly, there is unequivocal evidence that many of these are linked to one and the same man", and Rachel let the information on the table sink in for a while.

- 28 years ago: Innsbruck, Austria; 11-year-old boy raped and murdered; DNA?
- 25 years ago: Berlin, Germany; 12-year-old boy raped and strangled; DNA?
- 25-15 years ago: Harbourtown, UK; remains of 9- to 13-year-old-boy found ('moorboy'); identity of victim not identified; ***DNA results available and basis for comparative analysis with other cases***
- 16 years ago: Morlaix, France; 11-year-old boy raped and strangled; ***DNA matches DNA result from 'moorboy' case***
- 14 years ago: Warsaw, Poland; 12-year-old boy raped and murdered; DNA?
- 13 years ago: Helsinki, Finland; 10-year old boy raped and murdered; DNA?
- 12 years ago: Madrid, Spain; 10-year-old boy raped and strangled; ***DNA matches DNA result from 'moorboy' case***

- 12 years ago: Bordeaux, France: 12-year-old boy raped and strangled; *DNA matches DNA result from 'moorboy' case*
- 11 years ago: Munich, Germany; 11-year-old boy raped and strangled; *DNA matches DNA result from 'moorboy' case*
- 11 years ago: Prague, Czech Republic; 9-year-old boy raped, strangled; boy's brutal rape had already severely injured the boy before he was strangled; DNA?
- 10 years ago: Amsterdam, The Netherlands; 10-year-old boy raped and strangled; *DNA matches DNA result from 'moorboy' case*
- 9 years ago: Brussels, Belgium; 11-year-old boy raped and strangled; *DNA matches DNA result from 'moorboy' case*
- 9 years ago: Copenhagen, Denmark; 12-year-old boy raped and strangled; *DNA matches DNA result from 'moorboy' case*
- 8 years ago: Riga, Latvia; 11-year-old boy raped and strangled; *DNA matches DNA result from 'moorboy' case*
- 8 years ago: Skopje, North Macedonia; 11-year-old boy raped and murdered; DNA?
- 6 years ago: Oslo, Norway; 11-year-old boy raped and strangled; *DNA matches DNA result from 'moorboy' case*

- 6 years ago: Antwerp, Belgium; 12-year-old boy raped and strangled; *DNA matches DNA result from 'moorboy' case*
- 5 years ago: Rome, Italy; 11-year-old boy raped and strangled; DNA?
- 5 years ago: Vienna, Austria; 11-year-old boy raped and strangled; *DNA matches DNA result from 'moorboy' case*
- 4 years ago: Budapest, Hungary: 12-year-old raped and murdered; DNA?
- 3 years ago: Ankara, Turkey; 11-year-old raped and strangled; DNA?
- 3 years ago: Athens, Greece; 11-year-old boy raped and strangled (with belt); *DNA matches DNA result from 'moorboy' case*
- 3 years ago: Warsaw, Poland; 11-year-old boy raped and strangled; *DNA matches DNA result from 'moorboy' case*
- 2 years ago: Tallinn, Estonia; 10-year-old raped and murdered; *DNA matches DNA result from 'moorboy' case*
- 23 months ago: Lisbon, Portugal; 11-year-old boy raped and murdered; *DNA matches DNA result from 'moorboy' case*
- 20 months ago: Geneva, Switzerland; 11-year-old raped boy raped and murdered; *DNA matches DNA result from 'moorboy' case*

- 18 months ago: Nürnberg, Germany; 11-year-old boy raped and strangled; ***DNA matches DNA result from 'moorboy' case***
- 15 months ago: Sarajevo, Bosnia-Herzegovina; 11-year-old boy raped and strangled; ***DNA matches DNA result from 'moorboy' case***
- 11 months ago: Tirana, Albania; 11-year-old boy raped and murdered; ***DNA matches DNA result from 'moorboy' case***

After a minute or so, allowing the delegates to take in information provided in the table, Stefan picked up their talk again. "I wish to highlight a few key points emerging from the data shown in the table", he said with as calm a voice as possible. He could see the sheer disgust in many faces in the audience after they had digested the facts presented in the table.

"First, the sheer size of the list is flabbergasting!", he said, pointing at the screen. "29 cases are listed here, suggesting that, if they are indeed all connected, we have one of the worst and most vicious serial killers in front of us that Europe, and indeed the world, has ever seen! Our preliminary label of 'European boy killer' was, therefore, spot on."

"Second", Rachel picked up the thread in their well-rehearsed presentation, "you can see that these cases span a time frame of nearly 30 years.

Although not all these cases can be associated with the same murderer as DNA results are often lacking, especially in the earlier cases, all these cases share similarities with regard to the nature of the rape and murder of these boys. Although there will, inevitably, be gaps and probably more similar cases will come to light over the next few months, we already have one of the biggest confirmed serial killer cases in front of us, because, thirdly, and as you can see from the items in bold in the table, of the 29 cases 20 show matching DNA! So, for 20 rapes and murders we already have confirmation that these were perpetrated by one and the same person!"

Rachel let this information sink in again. A gasp went through the audience.

"Unfortunately, the table does not allow us yet to say where the serial killer comes from and where he might be based. Although the first DNA match, indeed the DNA used as a baseline for all other comparisons, comes from my own 'moorboy' case and is probably the earliest DNA we have, I do not wish to jump to conclusions yet. As you can see from the table, we still are unable to identify who moorboy was and in what year he was killed. Several months after the find of the boy's skeleton, one of my colleagues is still struggling to match up the corpse we found with our list of missing boys, spanning several decades. This is why we have,

tentatively, put the timeframe for moorboy's case in the table as 25 to 15 years ago. This means that our moorboy case might just be one in a sequence of earlier cases, and there could be many more of these earlier cases we have not yet identified. Unfortunately this also means that it would be futile at this stage to embark on widespread DNA analyses of male populations in a certain area to identify the possible perpetrator. We don't even know which country the serial killer comes from."

Rachel briefly gathered her thoughts. It was evident that moorboy must have been one of the earlier victims of their serial killer, but how many more had there been before and would they ever be able to find out?

"And you can see that those cases mentioned by some of you at our last meeting", Rachel continued and glanced over at the Greek, French, Spanish, Belgian, Norwegian and Croatian colleagues in particular, "all showed DNA matches with our moorboy case in Harbourtown and Stefan's Nürnberg boy murder 18 months ago. All these boys have been raped and killed by the same man!"

A gasp could be heard from the audience. Several delegates glanced at each other and nodded, stunned by the findings.

"But", Rachel continued, "despite all our efforts and many police analysts in Europe now working on this case, we cannot find any match with existing

European DNA data banks. Our serial killer has no previous convictions."

Although Rachel and Stefan had already talked about this to many EIPT colleagues, the confirmation of this news nonetheless elicited another audible gasp from the delegates. They all knew that if the identity of the killer could not be found, the killing spree could continue unabated for years.

"Fourth", Stefan picked up their presentation again, "the table tells us a lot about the methodology of the serial killer. Although, as Rachel has said, the list is most certainly incomplete, we can see a certain regularity in the patterns shown here. Our rapist and murderer seems to aim to rape and kill about every three to four months, although maybe he has not always achieved this. You can see, for example, that no cases are reported from seven years ago. Is this because he had a break, or, maybe more likely, because he failed to find suitable victims? If the latter is the case, then he probably scouted out many more kids than we see here, and the table only shows the tip of the iceberg."

Another gasp went through the audience.

"In any case, we hope to hear more about the serial killer's methodology shortly, as Dr Sonderegger has kindly asked one of his colleagues, a criminal psychologist, to analyse the available

data and give us a preliminary psychological profile of the killer."

Dr Sonderegger nodded back while glancing at his mobile phone. "Prof Dr Schallenberg has just informed me that he is on his way", Sonderegger said with a nod back to Rachel and Stefan. "He was just held up in one of the other EIPT meetings where he was also asked to give his opinion, and he will be with us shortly."

"The temporal pattern over the past two years or so may be most revealing", Stefan continued. "Arguably we have the most detailed info over the past few years as these cases are all still open. You can see", and Stefan pointed at the last two years in the table, "that our perpetrator raped and killed boys with regularity every three months or so recently, including the Lisbon case 23 months ago, Geneva 20 months ago, and our own case in Nürnberg, now about 18 months back. And only three months later the rape and murder in Sarajevo, and then four months later in Tirana, Albania. But we have had no further reports since. So, is our serial killer having another break, or has he just not been able to find more victims lately? Is he possibly getting scared and more cautious? If not, then he must be getting pretty desperate to find another victim soon, judging from the pattern over the past 25 years or so."

Stefan and Rachel let this information sink in again. The certainly could see that their colleagues in the room were keen to hear the rest of their findings as they were all fixated on the screen.

"A fifth and sixth pattern has also been apparent, although we did not show this in the table", Rachel picked up their presentation again. "All cases reported so far took place in poor urban areas. By the way, this is why we have also included the first two cases in Innsbruck and Berlin in the table although we are unlikely to get DNA results for these old cases", Rachel said while pointing at the top of the table. "So, there is another pattern here: our serial killer wilfully selects kids from poor areas, maybe because the kids are less supervised there, or maybe because it is easier for him to hide? Almost all rapes and murders were committed in hiding places behind garages or in derelict buildings, away from view. This is much more difficult to do in well-to-do suburban areas with more effective neighbourhood watch systems and where kids can more easily be supervised by their parents while playing in front gardens or on the street. Another pattern might be – and we are still looking into this in more detail using *Geographic Information System* analysis – that all areas where the rapes and murders took place are not far from airports, i.e. at most 30 minutes by public transport if that is how our perpetrator gets around."

"This is why", Stefan stepped in, "I and my team have already started scouring all the passenger databases of airports in the cities listed in the table. What we are trying to find is whether one and the same name appears on the exact dates of the murders in each city on the passenger lists. You probably would think that in this day and age of supercomputers this should be an easy and quick task, but believe me it isn't. Budgets are an issue and, even with gratefully acknowledged financial help from both EIPT and *Interpol*, we have not yet managed to get access to all the necessary data for this task. But much more problematic is the fact that passenger data does not come in uniform shape, especially older data over ten years ago, so it is actually not easy at the moment to crunch the little data we have. So, what I am saying is that, while we are looking at this passenger data, it might still take a few months to come up with results."

The colleagues in the audience fully understood Stefan's frustration and nodded encouragingly.

The door opened and a slim, white-haired and white-bearded man walked in, nodding towards Sonderegger who stood up to shake the man's hand.

"May I present you Prof Dr Schallenberg", Sonderegger said to the audience, "a criminal psychologist colleague of mine, who, as mentioned earlier, has worked on a psychological profile of our 'European boy killer', and who has kindly agreed to

present his preliminary findings here. Please, Prof Schallenberg …", and Sonderegger led the professor towards the front where he shook hands with Rachel and Stefan.

"One last thing to mention", Rachel said while Schallenberg was getting ready for his presentation. "We have just had notification from our Russian colleagues in Moscow of a botched attack on an 11-year-old boy in the Moscow district of Somjenkowo, one of the poorest areas in that city. Although it is much too early to say whether this is indeed linked to our serial killer, many of the parameters we discussed also fit this case: a poor neighbourhood, an 11-year-old slim boy which seems to be our perpetrator's preferred targets, and an area not far from Moscow's main airport. According to Moscow police, the boy was able to see the man's face and a phantom drawing of the man's face will be sent to us shortly. If this is indeed our serial killer, to our knowledge this would be the first time that a boy has escaped from his clutches and is in a position to provide information about his attacker. Needless to say, we are closely following further developments here and will keep you informed as soon as we hear more."

"Finally", Stefan stepped forward, "we should also mention that we are pursuing yet another possible avenue for identification of our killer. Many of you will know that many ancestry websites

have sprung up in recent years all across the world, with many operating in Europe and the USA. This includes, for example, the Mormon-based ancestry website in the USA which is one of the most complete digital ancestry data sources in the world. Through the German Innenministerium, we are currently in discussion with the *European Court of Justice* whether exceptional access could be granted to these ancestry websites for our investigation of the European boy killer. Here, we are particularly interested in those websites and firms that offer DNA analysis for the purpose of tracing ancestry. Who knows, maybe with a bit of luck we can find a member of the serial killer's family somewhere in Europe which would substantially narrow down our search. It is still early days on this, and we are unsure whether access will be granted to what is strictly protected confidential DNA data, but, again, we will keep you informed of any further developments on this front."

Sonderegger thanked Rachel and Stefan for their presentation and gave the floor to Prof Schallenberg. With appreciative nods from their colleagues for all the hard work and insight they had provided, Rachel and Stefan sat down to listen to what the criminal psychologist had to say about their serial killer.

"Good afternoon and apologies that I could not be with you earlier, but, as Dr Sonderegger may

have already mentioned, I was also asked to give my expertise on another case currently discussed by EIPT. Mrs Sontheimer and Mr Scholz made available all their data and information weeks before this meeting which has allowed me to do a preliminary psychological evaluation of your perpetrator. I should say at the outset that my assessment is based on over three decades of expertise I have had, in particular with international serial killer cases, and that I have also worked in New York State in the USA for ten years as one of their criminal psychologist experts. So, where to begin …", and Schallenberg called up his first *PowerPoint* slide which summarised his key findings.

"Mrs Sontheimer's and Mr Scholz's intricate analysis of possible and definite rapes and murders associated with our serial killer allows me to make several assumptions. First, based on the timeline in question, our killer must be at least in his 30s, but maybe older, depending on when the first rape and murder took place. But, from past experience, serial killers usually start their killing sprees in their mid to late teens, and at the latest in their early 20s, so, I would say, that we are looking at a man who is about 30 to 45 years old. The timing of his rapes and murders is particularly instructive from a criminal psychology perspective: as you will have heard, there is a system and methodology to these cases

that suggests that our perpetrator requires regular sexual release through his actions. The three- to four-month intervals he has between his rapes and murders suggests maybe that he struggles to find other outlets for his sexual gratification. So, he could be a man who can only orgasm when raping young boys. One rape might sate his sexual lust for a while, but, as psychological and bodily needs build up, after a few months he needs to find another victim. The fact that he targets only young boys, mainly aged between 10 and 12, is a further revelation. The man clearly is only aroused by young boys, so we can fairly assume that he is not in a relationship with a woman or an adult man. Psychologically, the reasons for this are complex, and it is impossible for me to tell from the available data where this man's depraved sexual urge comes from, but, from past experience, it is likely that he was himself the victim of rape as a young boy, a fact that might also help in narrowing the circle of possible culprits once you are at a stage of drawing up a shortlist ...", Schallenberg said while looking particularly at Rachel and Stefan.

Rachel and Stefan found this incisive analysis very helpful and nodded back in acknowledgement. Although most of the issues the professor raised were probably common sense, his analysis would certainly help them to further establish a picture in their own minds about the perpetrator, what a

person he was, and what drove him to do what he did.

"In other words, I suspect that the monster we are seeking is just a mere reflection of who we are and of what society and his family have done to him", Schallenberg continued. "After all, all violence is rooted in shame, and shame is probably what defines this man's inability to arouse himself other than with young vulnerable boys. Shame as reflection of the response of his own body when he might have been raped himself as a young boy, shame that he could not fight the sexual pleasure he might have felt when he was being raped himself by his assailant. I would also assume that our serial killer, in addition to possibly being raped himself as a young boy by a parent or relative, also did not receive much love from his parents. Maybe his parents died and he was placed into care, a frequent and unfortunate upbringing for many who become serial killers. Or one or both of his parents were alcoholics or drug addicts and did not have the energy or interest to interact much with their son. Indeed, the child who has not received affection, the enabling love of the parent, can develop an anger and hatred of the world and may go over to the dark side."

Schallenberg paused briefly and flicked to the next *PowerPoint* slide. The audience were

completely silent and entranced by every word the professor said.

"The callous way he rapes and kills the boys is also revealing", Schallenberg continued. "There is evidence here of a psychopathic need for control. Psychopaths are rational people, they are not mentally ill, which means that they are fully in control of their actions. They plan ahead. But it is also about using helpless human beings, it is all about control, most likely control this man did not have when he was young. The depraved and callous approach he uses also suggests a complete failure to take responsibility for his actions, possibly also associated with what we call malignant narcissism. The man feels entitled, he feels he has the right to rape these young boys, maybe because the same had been done to him? The killing of the boys, by the way, is probably incidental. He has to kill them so as not to be identified, but the main driver for what he is doing is his sexual lust, the rapes. So our serial killer is only a murderer because he is forced by his sexual urge to kill. I would also imagine that a key driving force for his acts is preserving the memory of his acts: he probably relives his rapes over and over again, revisits the moment when he is all powerful, when he has full control over his hapless victims. I suppose that he does not dare take any mementoes from his rapes, pieces of clothing, for example, or take photos and films, as all these could

be used as evidence against him. But this methodology then also means that his memory of the rapes fades over time, and after three to four months he is in need of another rape, both to satiate his pent-up sexual lust but also to recharge his memory with a new act of rape." Schallenberg briefly paused and flicked to the next *PowerPoint* slide.

"What is also evident from the data", Schallenberg continued, "is that we are probably dealing with a highly intelligent man. Past evidence shows that many serial killers are very intelligent individuals, which is one of the reasons why they are often able to avoid being caught for so long. They are often meticulous planners, as seems also to be the case with our European boy killer. Clearly, this man has a clear plan and methodology: he rapes and kills in different countries and different cities; with a few exceptions he avoids raping and killing in the same country; and he chooses large anonymous cities and places where people tend not to look after their kids as well as, say, in small villages in the countryside with usually tighter-knit communities. And he has knowledge of what criminologists call 'linkage blindness' – I think this has already been mentioned in the context of this case here at EIPT meetings …?", Schallenberg asked while glancing at Sonderegger who nodded back in acknowledgement.

"Again, this shows that this man is not just driven by sheer lust and instinct, he is a clever, calculating man who is trying to fool police forces in their countries by making them think that their young boy rape and murder cases are unique and one-off incidences that do not need to be contextualised internationally. And it is only thanks to the foresight, or maybe sheer luck, of our two detectives here ...", and he nodded towards Rachel and Stefan who nodded back, honoured to be mentioned so positively, "that the international connections of this case could be identified. And what a trove of depravity across the whole of Europe they uncovered!"

Schallenberg dabbed some perspiration from his forehead. He recomposed himself and picked up the thread again. "So, to me, this is, therefore, an individual who has access to resources and possibilities to travel regularly to different European destinations. It could be somebody with a job that allows a lot of freedom, and good excuses, to travel without eliciting any suspicion among his peer group. It could, for example, be a self-employed person or a millionaire with plentiful funds who would not arouse suspicion with all this travel. If it is an employed person, I am thinking here about jobs such as journalists or other media jobs, maybe a businessman, or possibly an academic. Being an academic and a professor

myself at the University of Basel in Switzerland, I know how much freedom and time some academics have to go to workshops and conferences, and many of us are lucky enough to have research budgets that pay for all these travel expenses."

Again, Schallenberg paused for a few seconds. He ruffled in his notes to see whether there was anything he had forgotten, but he seemed to be satisfied that he had said all he wanted to say.

"So, although I cannot tell you more about this individual and especially where he comes from, we have here in front of us a very frustrated and unhappy man who is happy to sink to the lowest levels of depravity to satisfy his debased sexual urges. He is probably somebody who lives alone, without a girlfriend, wife, or partner. He is in a job or position that allows him a lot of freedom to travel, and he is a calculating and well-planned man that uses all possibilities to evade being caught. In fact, he is so sure about his methodology that he does not hesitate to leave the most personal information about himself inside the boys' bodies: his semen. This latter fact supports the notion that we are dealing with a man who is sure about what he is doing, who is certain that he will never be caught, and who uses the fact that nation states are still focused more on rapes and murders within their national boundaries without much opportunity for transnational collaboration. I, therefore, highly

commend what EIPT are trying to achieve here and wish you the best of luck with capturing this evil monster. Please do not hesitate to lean on my expertise for any further analysis of this case, and I thank all of you for asking me to be involved. Thank you."

Sonderegger stood up, walked towards Schallenberg and vigorously shook Schallenberg's hand. This broad-based, yet incisive, dissection of the serial killer's persona was exactly what their meeting had hoped for. Stefan and Rachel were also very pleased with Schallenberg's witty analysis. Rachel now saw the shapes of a man emerging in her mind, a vicious middle aged serial killer, a depraved but intelligent man who would do everything to avoid capture. She was also certain that many more young boys in Europe were in grave danger of becoming this monster's next victim. More than ever she was convinced that they had to act fast, and devote all their energy to capture this rapist and murderer. Maybe they needed a bit of luck again, but she knew deep inside that this meeting had brought them just one step closer.

23

The present

It had been a few days since Pascal had escaped from home. He was still living in the old derelict factory and had, at least so far, not been bothered by anybody. Lying on the hard concrete floor, he shifted uncomfortably inside his sleeping bag. Although he wore all the clothes he had brought with him, he was still cold, even inside the sleeping bag. Pascal put his arms inside the bag and held up the edges of the bag to his chin. But the bag was not long enough for him to put his head inside and it was his head that felt particularly cold. Pascal exhaled with a loud hiss and could see his breath dissipating in the huge factory hall.

His torch had perceptibly dimmed over the past hour, it needed new batteries. The torch barely illuminated the immediate surroundings of Pascal's makeshift bed, all around him Pascal felt the overwhelming presence of the dark void of the large factory hall. Although the weather had been dry for days, water was still dripping from the ceiling nearby. There were also constant unnerving noises emanating from the old, rusty machines all around him in the dark, the tingling of a chain in a faint

breeze, the rustling of a mouse or rat hurrying through a maze of cables, the creaking of a door or hatch somewhere to his left. Pascal was scared. He hated this place and did not sleep well in this scary, dark void, his sleep constantly interrupted by noises. Pascal knew that the police or the children's social services were looking for him and that it would only be a matter of time until they found him. Of course, they would soon hear about the kid who stole food from nearby market stalls and grocery shops. Only just yesterday had he just managed to escape from the clutches of the Algerian shop keeper around the corner, after stealing some apples and bananas.

And he did not know whether his father had survived his latest mind-sucking attack. Not that he cared much about his father, nor his mum to that effect, but he still wanted to know whether his dad was still alive. But he could not dare go near his flat for fear of being caught, nor could he go back to school where the authorities surely waited for him. Pascal could feel despair growing again in him, this feeling of dread he'd had ever since escaping from home. Still holding his sleeping bag up to his chin for warmth, Pascal started sobbing loudly. Although he wanted to be strong, to be stoic, to show himself that he was able to cope now at the age of 11, these crying spells kept overwhelming him. He felt so lonely, so desperate! But what could

he do? Although his stomach rumbled from hunger, he slowly cried himself to sleep, the nearby drip-drip of water receding into the distance …

24

The present

Kevin woke up with a jolt, covered in sweat. He could feel the familiar stickiness between his legs of another wet dream. It must have just happened, as his penis still felt stiff and erect. Kevin switched on his bedside light and pushed away his duvet. He slept in t-shirt and underpants, and a large wet patch was clearly visible at the front of his pants. He yanked off his underpants and wiped the sticky and moist sperm from his testicles and inner thighs. His erection had abated and Kevin stared at his limp and shrivelled penis. How he hated this appendage that dictated his entire life, that led him to do to boys what he had been doing for the past 20 years, and that nonetheless had a complete will of its own, not letting him touch it or masturbate like all other men his age without a regular partner. Why would his penis not allow him to release himself? Why did it not work?

Of course, Kevin had thought long and hard over the past 20 years why he was unable to masturbate. He was a bright man and had read some books about psychology and sexual problems. Of course he knew that it was linked to his childhood

trauma with Keith, of being raped himself, of feeling completely out of control when he had first orgasmed while Keith had molested him. He knew all that, and yet he could still not command his own penis to respond to his own caresses and stroking. Kevin also knew that things probably would have been very different had he been able to masturbate. At least this would have given him some escape, some safety valve, some release, from this terrible sexual tension that was constantly building up.

The feeling of satisfaction, of fulfilment, of happiness of raping of a boy, usually lasted three or four months in which he would play the scene of the rape in his mind over-and-over again. But then the memories tended to fade, the initial crystal-clear detail of his penis penetrating the boy's anus, the thrusting, the wonderful orgasm inside the boy, gradually faded, almost as if the images dissolved in a fog. And after a while only snippets, fragments, shards of the original memories remained. To be sure, the only occasion where one of his rape victims had actually orgasmed – the boy in Geneva 16 months ago – continued to be fresh in Kevin's mind. This only occasion where a boy had been aroused by Kevin still stood out as something very special. But it made Kevin cringe even more in despair as he knew that this powerful memory would also soon fade into the distant recesses of his mind.

And now this dreadful patch of botched rape attempts in Ljubljana and Moscow. The rape in Tirana, Albania, now 13 months ago, was the last time he had found sexual release with a boy. Over a year! Of course his pent-up sexual pressure needed to find other ways of release, which was one of the reasons why these dreadful and highly unsatisfactory wet dreams appeared to be occurring with growing frequency. This was not what Kevin wanted. He needed another boy victim! And very soon! His sexual frustration was driving him mad.

Although it was still early in the morning and dark outside, Kevin got up. All this thinking about his latest wet dream and his growing sexual frustration had made further sleep impossible. With a tissue he wiped the sperm from his bedsheet. With a disgusted look on his face he discarded the tissue into the toilet bowl. He hated the fact that he had to do this, he hated his body … and he hated himself. Severely depressed and with the darkest thoughts on his mind, Kevin made his way to the living room. He did not switch on the light and instead gazed out of the floor-to-ceiling windows over Harbourtown marina and harbour stretching out in front of him. Hundreds of luxury yachts were moored alongside winding quays. The water inside the marina was dead still, and the reflection of a half-moon was visible in the water, occasionally blurred by the hint of a ripple caused by the slightest of breezes.

But Kevin did not enjoy the view. His flat was a purely functional thing for him. It contained nothing personal, no pictures on the wall, no mementoes from his many trips, no memories of his mum or family. It was sterile and almost barren of furniture. His kitchen contained only the most necessary items, there was nothing superfluous in his flat. It was only a place for waiting … for waiting for the next boy rape. And only coincidentally was it located in one of Harbourtown's most picturesque areas – one of the few areas not ravaged by German bombing raids in the Second World War and maintaining a bustling, rustic charm that was so lacking from other areas of impoverished and decrepit Harbourtown.

But instead of gazing out of the window, Kevin turned away and thought, again, about suicide. This was certainly not the first time he thought about killing himself, about putting an end to his miserable and depraved life. This was not out of sympathy for future boy victims – he could not care less about future lives he would inevitably be forced to take – but it was only for himself: to end his suffering, his sexual frustration, his meaningless life. These suicidal feelings became particularly acute after long spells of sexual inactivity, and, apart from the time when he was a teenager, the past 13 months had been one of the longest spells without raping a boy. This meant that,

psychologically and emotionally, Kevin was at the end of his tether. He needed another boy, he needed sexual release as soon as possible.

Luckily, his next conference on resilience was only a few weeks away. He counted the days until his next trip. He could not wait! At least this prospect of raping another boy soothed his anguished and dark mind a little bit, and his suicidal feelings abated at least for the moment. In a slightly lighter mood, Kevin walked into the kitchen, switched on the light, and started the coffee machine.

25

The present

Rachel snuggled up to Stefan who was lying next to her in the large king-sized bed. Stefan had come to see her in Harbourtown for the first time. They had enjoyed a few relaxing days together, with frequent lovemaking, regular strolls around Harbourtown harbour, and drinking coffee in Rachel's favourite coffee bar by the marina every day. Rachel had taken a few days off work so that she could concentrate fully on Stefan's visit. After her recent breakthrough in finding out that the moorboy case was in fact not an isolated incident but that it was linked to a serial killer, and after glowing feedback from the EIPT about how she and Stefan were helping with the coordination of the search for the 'European boy killer', Superintendent Warrington had not hesitated to allow Rachel some well-deserved time off.

But, Rachel being Rachel and a dedicated and fully-focused police inspector, she could, of course, never fully relax. And neither could Stefan who had been equally obsessed with the European boy killer case from the moment they had realised there was a link between the two boy murders in their respective

jurisdictions. This had meant that Stefan and Rachel had talked almost incessantly about the serial killer.

Rachel looked at the phantom drawing again which had recently been emailed to all EIPT committee members by their Moscow colleagues. The drawing was based on evidence provided by the 11-year-old boy from the poor Moscow district of Somjenkowo who had escaped the attempt of a man who had attempted to rape and kill him. Rachel glanced at the drawing which showed the haggard face of a man in his early- to mid-thirties, with a well-proportioned nose, dark eyebrows, a clean-shaven face, and dark brown hair that partly covered his ears and that looked a bit dishevelled at the top. But what struck Rachel most were the eyes of the man shown in the drawing. She was unsure whether it was just a quirk of the light of her bedside table or just how the expert drawer at the Moscow police department had captured them, but the man's eyes were dark, menacing and piercing. Rachel felt a shiver running down her spine as she glanced into these dark eyes, and she had the impression that the man in the drawing stared straight at her, inside her, and dissected her soul with his menacing look.

Rachel suddenly felt cold in her nakedness and snuggled up more closely to Stefan who held her more tightly. Was this the man they were looking for? Was this the man who decades ago had raped and strangled moorboy and who had recently raped

and killed the boy in Nürnberg and all these other boys in European cities? Could it be him?

"If this picture is accurate, then this man may have been very young when he killed moorboy", Rachel mused while turning her head towards Stefan who also stared at the drawing with undisguised fascination.

"Indeed, and he would have been really young if he is the one who raped and killed the boys in Innsbruck 28 years ago and Berlin 25 years ago, as per our list of boy rapes and murders", Stefan replied. They both knew that it was still difficult to fit the moorboy case into a neat temporal sequence, as neither the victim nor the exact date of the murder had been identified yet.

Rachel stared back at the drawing. Somewhere in Europe this man still walked freely, and probably planned his next attack on a boy at this very moment. She knew that they had to do everything they could to stop him. She and Stefan had already talked at length about the other strands of their investigation, which had started after the last EIPT meeting. Stefan had made considerable progress about accessing and disentangling airport passenger data for the cities on their list of boy murders, and he just waited to hear the results from this part of their enquiry from colleagues back in Germany.

Their request through both EIPT and *Interpol* to obtain access to DNA data of millions of people

who had sent in samples to ancestry websites also looked promising. Although all the ancestry internet businesses they had contacted were adamant that they could not breach client confidentiality, as this was the key ingredient of their business model, the *European Court of Justice* had agreed a few weeks earlier that there were enough grounds just for this specific case to exceptionally allow EIPT and *Interpol* access to the vast confidential DNA data stores of these firms, on the understanding that this data would be used for this case only and that this request would not open the floodgates to others interested in these DNA archives.

All ancestry sites had to reluctantly agree to the request by the *European Court*, and, as a result, the DNA results from the serial killer's semen had already been sent to these firms for comparison. Rachel had also sent the DNA results of moorboy himself, in the faint hope that one of moorboy's relatives might have sent in a DNA sample for ancestral analysis. They had already received notifications back from several of these firms that, if indeed relatives of both moorboy and the serial killer had sent in DNA samples, matching these samples with those of moorboy or the serial killer would not take long. Stefan was optimistic that they should obtain results any day now. Of course, they both knew that a positive result relied on the fact that close relatives of both moorboy and the

European boy killer had sent in their DNA for analysis of their ancestry. If that was not the case, then they would have to start again from scratch.

Rachel put the phantom drawing back on her bedside table. After all, she was on holiday and she needed time off from the case, even if this was not easy with Stefan at her side who constantly wanted to talk about progress on the case with her.

She snuggled up closer to him and pressed the pause button of her Sky control to continue the movie they were watching, which Rachel had saved on her Skybox. It was *Silence of the Lambs*, the 1992 cinematographic masterpiece by Jonathan Demme and still Rachel's favourite crime thriller. The night before, just before going to sleep, they had reached the scene in the movie where agent Clarice Starling had gone down into the basement of the prison where psychopath Hannibal Lecter was held in his glass-fronted cell. Some of the most iconic and oft-quoted lines from that movie were uttered by Hannibal in precisely this scene. Although both Rachel and Stefan had seen the movie several times before, they were nonetheless glued to the screen when Hannibal approached the glass wall of his cell and stared into Agent Starling's scared face with his cold steely-grey eyes while uttering the famous line: "First principles, Clarice, first principles. Of each particular thing ask: what is it in itself? What is its nature? What

does he do, this man you seek? We begin by coveting what we see every day".

Something in Rachel's mind suddenly clicked, but she could not quite see what it was. Could this sentence, uttered by one of the most iconic screen villains have something to do with their case? She was unsure and carried on watching the gruesome scenes of the movie unfold in front of them. But when, just a few minutes later, agent Starling sees Hannibal's note to her about the geographical location of the murders that says "Clarice, doesn't this random scattering of sites seem desperately random? Like the elaborations of a bad liar?", Rachel paused the movie immediately.

She and Stefan looked at each other. Both had realised the same thing at the same time. It was as if a switch had been flicked on and a sudden realisation, an instantaneous epiphany, had hit them at exactly the same time. Still naked and not bothering to put on any clothes, they both rushed to Rachel's kitchen table where they rummaged through the papers on the European boy killer lying in a heap in front of them. Almost simultaneously, they pulled out the sheet with the table of the murders from the pile.

"Of course!", Rachel exclaimed, jumping up and down with excitement. "We had it in front of our eyes all the time, and yet we could not see it! How stupid we have been!"

Stefan seemed to have come to the same realisation. "Indeed", he replied. "If we look at the pattern of murders in front of us, one really stands out as being different. Other people in EIPT would probably not see this as they don't know enough about the cases, but to you and me it should have been clear as soon as we drew up the list that one case really stood out: your moorboy case!"

"Yes!", Rachel picked up Stefan's line of reasoning. "If this list is reasonably complete – and we have to assume that it is – moorboy is the only one who was *buried* by our serial killer. None of the other boys had been buried. After raping them the killer strangled them and just left them lying where he had killed them. There was no attempt at hiding the other bodies."

"So, why would he bury moorboy and not the others?", Stefan asked, looking at Rachel. "Because", both said in unison, "first principles, Clarice, first principles. Of each particular thing ask: what is it in itself? What is its nature? What does he do, this man you seek? We begin by coveting what we see every day". They both laughed.

"And", Rachel continued, while pulling out a map showing the location of European boy killer's victims, "aren't all the sites where our European boy killer has murdered his victims 'desperately'

random, as Hannibal Lecter suggested in 'Silence of the lambs'?"

"It is clear what this means", Stefan replied with a sudden calmness in his voice that confirmed that they might have made a major breakthrough in this case. "Moorboy must have been our killer's first victim! Our timeline already hinted at that, but we were unsure as we have no precise date for the moorboy murder. But the fact that our killer buried him suggests that the murdered boy was somebody he knew, somebody near him ... And that the first two cases on our list, Innsbruck and Berlin, where we also have no DNA results for comparison, are probably not linked to our killer."

"The killer is somebody from Harbourtown!", Rachel continued Stefan's train of thought and with the sudden realisation of what this meant. "And must be somebody who lived or was based not far from where the killing of moorboy took place. Our serial killer is from here ... from Harbourtown! And maybe from somewhere near the spot where we found moorboy. That's why he has never killed in England again. That's why he has so desperately scattered all his murders across Europe. To deflect us from identifying him as somebody from Harbourtown, the site of his first killing, in case the buried body of moorboy would ever be found and identified. He had to bury his first victim as the discovery of the boy would have immediately

linked him to the murder. Whereas in the rest of Europe he did not care, as he rightly assumed that individual police forces would never make the link to the moorboy case, or to any of the other European cases we have identified. As you suspected along, our intelligent and cunning murderer has used this 'linkage blindness' to the best effect … and it has worked for him, not only for years but for decades."

"You know what this means", Stefan said, standing up, still naked, with his penis dangling not far from Rachel's face. "You need to start a search of this man here immediately. OK, a lot of time has passed since the moorboy murder, but, who knows? The killer may still be here. He might have lived not far from your police headquarters all these years, unperturbed, going about his depraved business of raping and killing young boys all across Europe. He certainly lived not far from here when moorboy was murdered all these decades ago."

Rachel realised that she had to contact Sergeant Inzuman Patel as soon as possible and discuss the implications of their new insights with him. Poor Inzuman! He had continued to be frustrated by the fact that he had still, after several months of enquiry, not been able to identify moorboy. The fact that the killer probably knew the boy would, finally, allow them to narrow down their search considerably.

It was nearly 1am, and Rachel knew that they could not do anything before the Harbourtown police headquarters reopened in the morning. She also knew that her little holiday had come to an abrupt halt.

26

The present

"This is incredible news!", Sergeant Patel exclaimed enthusiastically. Together with Superintendent Warrington and Inzuman Patel, Rachel and Stefan were crammed into Rachel's small office where they had relayed their new suspicions to their colleagues. Warrington and Patel had briefly wondered why Stefan was there in person and why he and Rachel had arrived together, but decency prevented them from enquiring further. They both knew that Rachel's complicated love life was none of their business.

"If it is true that the murderer knew moorboy and that he might have been quite young, possibly still a teenager, when he murdered the boy, then I can finally narrow down my search to the immediate vicinity of where moorboy was found and to people associated with that location. Upon hearing all this, my first hunch would be that both the murderer and moorboy came from Harbourtown College which is located less than a kilometre from where moorboy's body was found. Remember, Rachel, that we followed this line of enquiry at the beginning, but that we got stuck because of the

sheer number of missing boys in south-west UK we had to investigate and the fact that we could not identify moorboy's identity."

They were interrupted by Stefan's mobile phone ringing. Stefan answered and put it on speakerphone so that they all could hear the conversation.

"Hi Stefan", a German-sounding voice said. "We have the result from your airport passenger manifest analysis."

Rachel, Stefan, Inzuman and Warrington huddled closer together around Rachel's table so that they could better hear what Stefan's colleague was about to tell them.

"Although it took us a while to obtain the data from all the airports located in cities where the European boy killer raped and killed", Stefan's colleague continued, "and to transcribe some of the older data into a format that could be more easily analysed and compared, we have a fairly clear result. We are still missing data from six of the 29 locations mentioned in the table you gave us, but we were able to get data from your first two, Innsbruck and Berlin and most of the others. Your third case in the table, Harbourtown, could, of course, not be used as this is the only one where we do not have an exact date for the murder, and some locations in Eastern Europe have still not been able to send us

any meaningful data. But we thought that we have enough information already to contact you."

Rachel and the others leaned further forward, eager to hear the result.

"Of course", Stefan's colleague continued, "our analysis is based on the assumption that our killer was, first, using planes to leave the city after he had just committed another rape and murder, and, second, that he used his own name, or the same fake name, on all these flights. But based on what Stefan told me, your killer left his DNA in the form of semen inside the boys without any attempt to hide his identity, so we can probably safely assume that he did the same about using his own real name. As you mentioned in your EIPT report, the killer has felt so confident that 'linkage blindness' would not enable all his crimes across Europe to be connected, and that he probably saw no need to hide his identity when he booked his flights."

Rachel and the others leaned even further forward. Would there be a meaningful result from this strand of their investigation?

"And, indeed, only one name appeared more than once on the passenger manifesto of all these flights we analysed that occurred within a timespan of about eight hours from the murders of the boys. I should also mention that probability theory suggests that the random chance of the same person to appear on the manifesto of more than one flight is basically

zero, which means that we are pretty sure that this is the man we are looking for. His name is Kevin Miller, a British citizen, and his name appears on *all* the flights we looked at, except for the first two in Innsbruck and Berlin, and we also have no link with one of the first murders in Morlaix in Brittany. For the latter case we have matching DNA evidence, but here we have to assume that Miller did not fly to that location."

For a brief moment, Rachel and the others said nothing. They were all surprised at how clear-cut the result from the airport passenger list was.

"Kevin Miller!", Rachel uttered, breaking the spell. "Never heard of him. And what an ordinary sounding name for someone who might have killed and raped nearly thirty boys!", she said, echoing what the others were probably thinking.

"Based on the information about the time of the boy murders", Stefan's colleague continued, "it appears that Miller boarded the first flights back home as soon as possible after he committed his crimes. Pretty much all his flights went back to London, or in some cases Bristol, confirming that he probably lives in the UK, possibly in the south-west of the country. In some instances he had to fly to another European transit airport first before flying on to the UK. We have checked all this, and, again, all the information matches up. Information about the last known boy murder 13 months ago, for

example, confirms this: Kevin Miller flew back from Tirana to Vienna, and then directly from Vienna to London."

"Many thanks", Stefan replied, "this confirms the theory we had all along that the sites of the murders were chosen by Kevin Miller as they were close to airports and, therefore, easy to escape from before the boy's bodies were found. This is evidently one of the reasons why he has been so careless about leaving his semen inside the boys, as he always knew that he would long be out of the country when his victims were eventually found. He was also confident that his DNA would only be compared with the available DNA evidence in the country where the rape and murder had taken place, but not with cases from beyond that country. What a cunning and calculating bastard! And it also seems to confirm that our first two cases on the list, Innsbruck and Berlin, might not be linked to our serial killer."

Stefan thanked his German colleague profusely. They immediately turned to Inzuman who ruffled through his papers to see whether a match could be found in any of his evidence of a Kevin Miller.

Rachel's mobile phone rang. This time it was from their French EIPT colleague who was helping to coordinate information sent by the ancestry website firms. Rachel smiled at her colleagues

about the coincidental timing of this call and put her phone on speakerphone.

"Bonjour Rachel, ça va?", the French colleague inquired.

"Oui merci Chantal, avez-vous des nouvelles?", Rachel replied, dredging up some of her French knowledge from long-past French lessons at school.

"Yes, I have news to report", Chantal replied.

"That's great, Chantal", Rachel replied. "Coincidentally, we have also just had excellent news from our airport passenger manifest analysis and we have a possible name for our serial killer."

"That is interesting", Chantal retorted, "let's see whether what I will tell you matches the info you already have. We have now heard back from four of the six ancestry websites that operate in Europe, and we have breakthrough info from the fourth firm, which is why I contact you now. First of all, we have a possible match with the DNA sample of the killer you sent us. There is a 12.5% match of the DNA with that of a person called Victoria Rowland who sent in a DNA sample for ancestral analysis to the site three years ago. Although 12.5% does not sound like much, i.e. she is for example not the sister or mother of our killer, 12.5% nonetheless suggests that she is a cousin of our killer, so still pretty close in terms of family linkages. According to the confidential info sent to us by this site, on the agreed understanding that this info can only be used

in the context of this case, Victoria lives in Bristol in the UK, so not that far from where you are Rachel."

"Now that is really exciting news, Chantal", Rachel replied enthusiastically. "The name we have identified through our flight passenger analysis is Kevin Miller. Can you see any link to this name in what you have found out about Victoria?"

"OK, just a moment", Chantal said. They could hear a few clicking sounds while Chantal pressed keys on her computer. "Yes, here it is. Victoria has posted a family tree on this ancestral website and the name Kevin Miller appears as one of her cousins. The site shows that Kevin never submitted his DNA for analysis – if he is indeed our murderer he would of course be foolish to do so – but he could, obviously not prevent his close relatives from doing so, and probably does not know that his cousin sent in her DNA to this site. Kevin is Victoria's 1st cousin. He is the son of Victoria's mother's sister, who is Kevin's mum. So, Kevin's mother was called Sheryl Rowland before she married a man called Miller. But I don't have more info on Kevin's side of the family through the website as Kevin's direct family – i.e. mother or father, he had no siblings – never sent their DNA analysis to this site."

Rachel glanced at the other three in the room. They were all smiling. Here they had direct

confirmation that the airport passenger list information was now directly linked to the DNA found in the victims. Kevin Miller was now definitely confirmed as the serial killer.

"And one more thing", Chantal continued. "Rachel, your colleague … Hazel Molfese … had also sent us the DNA from your buried boy victim, the boy you call 'moorboy'. There is also a match here from one of the other ancestry-site-firms."

In her excitement, Rachel had almost forgotten that moorboy's DNA had also been sent for comparison.

"Here we have a 25% match, so this person, a German man called Heinz Schlesinger, must be the uncle of your victim. Your moorboy, therefore, has a very strong German connection and might have been German himself …"

Upon hearing these last words, Sergeant Inzuman Patel had rushed to another pile of paper in front of him. After a few seconds he found what he was looking for.

"Look Rachel, here it is", he said with a beaming smile. "There is a boy called Markus Schlesinger on my long list of missing boys in the south-west of England, and this one is specifically from Harbourtown. I had looked at this boy's case right at the beginning but dismissed it as they boy was still just listed as 'missing' and no further info was available in the files. Maybe now we know why

this case was not further investigated at the time. Maybe the boy's parents had only been in the UK briefly and went back to Germany? Maybe that also explains why this case barely featured in the local news as the boy might not have lived in Harbourtown for long?"

Inzuman ruffled further through his papers. "And here it is", he said holding up triumphantly a crumpled sheet which contained a long alphabetic list of names of kids who had been to school at Harbourtown College ten to thirty years ago. "Both the name of Markus Schlesinger, Year 1, and Kevin Miller, Year 3, appear for the time exactly 20 years ago. Now we have confirmation that moorboy was Markus Schlesinger and that he was killed by his older schoolmate Kevin Miller 20 years ago."

Rachel thanked Chantal who had also heard Inzuman's revelations through the speakerphone. "This confirms what Stefan and I told you earlier", she said, addressing the other three in the room. "That Kevin knew Markus and that this was the reason he buried the body. Markus was indeed Kevin's first victim."

"But if Kevin was in Year 3 when he killed Markus …", Warrington chipped in, "then that makes him only about 14-years-old when he committed his first murder?"

A hush went through the room. Rachel had not had time to process all the information they had

been getting over the past hour or so, and only now did it dawn on her how young Kevin must have been when he first raped and murdered a boy. What depraved 14-year-old could commit such a crime? What had society, Kevin's family, the world, done to this boy that he would commit such an atrocious crime at such a young age? It was almost unthinkable.

"Surely this, together with the passenger manifesto information, then also confirms that the first two cases on our list could not have been committed by Kevin Miller", Stefan picked up their thread of thoughts. "Kevin would only have been a young boy of 6 and 9 years when the Innsbruck and Berlin murders occurred and, therefore, has to be ruled out as the perpetrator of these crimes. At least we now also have certainty that moorboy … sorry, Markus Schlesinger, was his first victim."

To Rachel, the next step was eminently clear. She swivelled her creaking chair around and tapped the name 'Kevin Miller' into the Google search engine. The site showed a long list of 'Kevin Millers' from all over the world, many in America, but at the bottom of the first page one line immediately struck her. Inzuman and Stefan had joined her and stood behind her to look at the screen. The last Google line read 'Kevin Miller, lecturer in Geography, Harbourtown University'. Rachel clicked on the line and Kevin Miller's

university website opened in front of them. A photo of Kevin was pinned in the top left corner of his site. What struck Rachel immediately was the steely and menacing look in Kevin's dark eyes, the same look she had seen in the phantom drawing just the night before! She grabbed the phantom drawing from Moscow from her bag and compared it with the photo of Kevin Miller in front of her. It was the same man! The same haggard face of a man in his mid-thirties, the same well-proportioned nose, the same dark eyebrows, the same clean-shaven face, and the same dark brown hair, slightly shorter on the university photo but unmistakably of the same person as on the drawing. Rachel was impressed at how close the phantom drawing came to the real man's appearance and how well the Moscow boy had remembered the face of his assailant. They could now also safely add the recent attempted rape in Moscow to the long list of Kevin Miller's victims.

Rachel immediately instructed Inzuman to ring the Geography Department at Harbourtown University to ask for Kevin Miller's home address and to enquire whether he was in his office this morning. But she also told Inzuman to be as inconspicuous as possible so as not to alert Kevin that the police were after him.

"He was right here at our doorstep all the time!", Rachel said while standing up and staring at Stefan

with a look of desperation on her face. "The bastard was here at the university right next door all the time! And we searched all over Europe for him and he was right here! I just can't believe it!"

Stefan placed a consoling hand on Rachel's shoulder, making both Warrington and Inzuman briefly cast furtive glances towards them. "And we have further confirmation that Kevin's job as an academic, as a geographer, gave him the best excuse to travel all over Europe, probably disguising his trips as 'research', while his real motive was to scout out young boy victims to rape and kill. What a monster! And of course being an academic confirms that we are dealing with a highly intelligent and well-planned serial killer who managed to hide his crimes for years. We will have to be extremely cautious when we go to apprehend him."

"I have the address!", Inzuman shouted, still holding the phone. "He is not in his office this morning, and the secretary was unsure whether Kevin Miller is away again on one of his many research trips, but I have his private address".

Rachel grabbed her firearm from the top left drawer of her desk and put on her bullet-proof west while handing another one to Stefan. She rarely wore the vest, but she knew that the confrontation with Kevin Miller that was about to come made it

imperative that they came well prepared and armed. A monster like Kevin was capable of anything!

27

The present

The caretaker of the block of flats where Kevin Miller had his appartement had cautiously opened the door to Kevin's flat, and had then quickly made his way back down the stairs while glancing back over his shoulder at Rachel, Inzuman and two other police officers who stood in front of the open door. They all head their guns at the ready and wore bullet-proof vests for protection.

"This is the police!", Rachel shouted into the flat. "Mr Miller, we are coming in …".

Rachel and Inzuman entered the flat, covering each other as they had learned at the police training academy so many years ago. The door opened onto a short hallway with two closed doors left and right and what looked like a spacious living room in front of them. Brandishing her weapon in front of her, Rachel cautiously opened the left door. Kevin's empty bedroom lay in front of her. While Inzuman covered her in the hallway, Rachel quickly inspected the room. What struck her first was how spartan the room was, with only one bed and a bedside table with a light and a built-in wardrobe near the window. The bed was immaculately made,

nothing was lying around, the room was almost sterile and devoid of any personality. Rachel quickly inspected the en-suite bathroom and toilet and checked the shower. "All clear" she shouted back to Inzuman after she had satisfied herself that Kevin could not hide anywhere in this constrained space.

Rachel quickly left the room and followed Inzuman who opened the right door which led into the kitchen. Again, no sign of Kevin. Like the bedroom, the kitchen was immaculately clean, with no dirty dishes or other items lying around. All cupboards were closed, every item was in its place, it almost looked as if the kitchen had never been used. The floor and surfaces were spotlessly clean.

Meanwhile the two other police officers had made their way into the living room and shouted "all clear". Rachel and Inzuman quickly joined them in the large, spacious and light living room. Again, the room was immaculately clean and spartan, with just one armchair to the right, a TV on the wall and an empty table in the middle of the room with just one chair. The view from the large floor-to-ceiling windows was stunning, with Harbourtown marina and harbour unfolding in front of them and the large millionaires' yachts bobbing in the calm harbour waters below them.

Seeing Kevin's flat confirmed to Rachel what psychologist Dr Schallenberg had hinted at during

his analysis of the serial killer at the last EIPT meeting. Kevin's flat revealed a lot about his personality. The flat was purely functional, it contained nothing personal, no family pictures on the wall, no mementoes from Kevin's many trips, nothing that would give a visitor an insight into the man's mind. The flat was sterile and barren and contained nothing superfluous. It was a serial killer's place for waiting, for biding his time, until the next rape and murder. It was like a hiding hole, a cave, a bunker from which Kevin Miller, the lethal predator of young innocent boys, would pounce when his depraved sexual urges overtook him again. Rachel imagined Kevin Miller like a large, ugly spider sitting in her net, waiting for the innocent victims to fall into her deadly fangs. She shivered and suddenly felt cold, despite the warm sunshine that basked the living room in a light and pleasant glow.

Rachel could well imagine that Kevin Miller rarely gazed out of the living room window to enjoy the view. This man was so entranced and obsessed by his sexual objective to rape young boys that nothing else seemed to matter to him. She wondered how he could concentrate on the difficult job of being an academic with all this sexual obsession driving him. But then, he was an intelligent man, and he could probably compartmentalise his life into his 'professional' persona and his 'rapist'

persona. But what would such a schizophrenic approach to life do to a person's mind? Standing in the man's living room, Rachel found it impossible to understand what drove Kevin Miller, his psyche, his desires and wishes. To her, he was like an alien, like an unpredictable animal, like a complete stranger whose priorities in life were so diametrically opposed to her own, to almost anybody else's lives, that these imperatives were impossible to understand for a sane person. She had to supress another shudder as she realised how much she hated and abhorred Kevin Miller. To her, he was Satan personified, beyond redemption, beyond evil.

"Kevin Miller's secretary was right", Rachel said to Inzuman with a sigh and conceding that, for now, Kevin Miller had escaped their clutches. "He must have left the country for one of his trips to Europe".

A panicked look from Inzuman confirmed what she was thinking. *Miller is on his way to kill another boy!*, Rachel thought with disgust. "We need to find out immediately from the Harbourtown Geography Department where he has gone, alert the authorities there with a picture of Miller and start a large-scale search", she said, while rushing Inzuman and the two police officers out of the flat. "Every second counts if we want to save another innocent boy's life!"

28

The present

Kevin was desperate. After such a long time without having raped a boy, he was not in a good frame of mind. His sexual lust was driving him to do things he would not have done in the past. He knew he was becoming reckless. His normally meticulous planning was in disarray, he realised that he was driven even more than usual by his penis than his brain.

He wiped the sweat from his forehead and looked behind him. He had finally lost his pursuers. *What a stupid idiot I am!*, he chided himself. *How could I be so reckless!* He had approached this beautiful Algerian-looking young boy in broad daylight out in the street without first scouting out the neighbourhood, checking it out for danger. And although the boy had, as usual, been willing to follow him for €20, Kevin had not realised that the boy's elder brothers had not been far away and watching the scene all the time. By the time he realised that he had made a terrible mistake, the two older teenagers were upon him and their younger brother, had snatched the boy from his hand, and had started shouting at Kevin and, when his answer

as to why he was escorting their brother away had not satisfied them, had threatened to beat him up.

Kevin had not hung around and had run away as fast as he could, but he was no match for two fit teenagers. They had quickly caught up with him, pushed him onto a patch of dirty grass strewn with dog turds and had started kicking him hard while swearing loudly in Arabic. Kevin had already thought that this was it, and had curdled up into a foetal position to ward off the heaviest blows when, luckily, and elderly lady walking her dog had marched towards them and, brandishing her umbrella, had somehow managed to distract the two boys' attention. Kevin had immediately used the opportunity and had run away, feeling a sharp pain in his sides from the beating he had received. While he ran, he had seen that the boys had managed to disengage themselves from the old lady and were running after him to complete their beating. Only by darting into an Algerian corner shop, running past the astonished owner, and, luckily, finding his way out through a back door that led to another road with a set of shops, had Kevin managed to get rid of his pursuers.

Peeping from behind shelves in a shop where he was hiding, Kevin glanced around him again. He could no longer see the two teenage boys. He could feel blood trickling down from his cut lip, and his

left side felt decidedly painful. Maybe the boys had broken one or several of his ribs?

His whole trip to Paris seemed to have been cursed. It had been such a rushed affair to organise the trip just after coming back from his disastrous trip to Moscow, to obtain a place in the resilience conference held at the *Université de Paris* at short notice, which, in turn, he needed to justify the trip expense through his research account at his university. But this time, Kevin had not even bothered to turn up at the conference. He had lost all interest he might have once had in questions of resilience, in research overall, and he now hated his job. The only thing he wanted was to satisfy his sexual lust, to find blissful release inside a young boy, any young boy, anywhere in Paris.

So, instead of attending the conference which was held in the *Marais* in one of the posher central parts of Paris, Kevin had immediately gone to the poor district of Branlieu situated not far from the main Paris airport from which he would fly home two days later. But then he had seen this beautiful slim and slender Algerian boy and his lust had taken over. Instead of carefully scouting out the place he had grabbed the boy and immediately had paid the price. He had been lucky that the old lady had distracted the boy's brothers, otherwise he would have probably ended up in hospital. And still, he was injured, he did not feel well.

Kevin peeped out of from behind the shelves again. He thought that the coast was clear, and ventured out of his hiding place. He opened the shop door and looked right and left down the bustling streets of Branlieu, but the two boys were nowhere to be seen. Relieved he made his way randomly to the left. He did not know exactly where he was, nor where he was going. *What is going on with you?*, he admonished himself again. *You are losing it! Keep it together! Just scout out an area, maybe locate a boy, and then go back to your hotel to clean up, ready for more scouting the next day, and then ... then rape a boy and fly back home. Just like you have done so many times before. C'mon Kevin ... !*

Kevin's aimless perambulation had taken him away from Branlieu's high street towards an even more derelict part of this dishevelled Paris suburb. Shops and dilapidated housing gave way to derelict factories and empty side streets full of rubbish and abandoned cars. Kevin realised that this was not the right place to spot 11-year-old boys and was about to turn back, when he suddenly saw him. About 50 metres away from Kevin, a young boy had just turned from the street into one of the abandoned factory buildings through a rusty steel door. Before entering, the boy had glanced suspiciously to his left and right as if not wanting to be spotted. Luckily, he had not spotted Kevin who had just stopped behind one of the abandoned car shells littering the side of

the street. The boy closed the rusty metal door behind him with a loud clang.

Kevin could not believe his luck. *What are you up to, little boy?*, he chuckled inwardly. *Maybe you have run away from home and are hiding in this abandoned building?* Kevin rubbed his hands in anticipation. He walked slowly towards the metal door behind which the boy had disappeared just seconds ago. Kevin glanced around him. The street was completely deserted, nobody was watching him. Carefully Kevin opened the door, very slowly to prevent it from clanging and creaking.

At first, Kevin found it hard to see in the dark, but some light filtered through cracks in both the walls and roof of the old factory building. Kevin stood in a large hall full of rusty old machines, cables dangling down from the ceiling, and he could hear water dripping from leaks in the corrugated iron roof. The place looked like it had been abandoned for years. For a moment, Kevin stood by the door and tried to see where the boy had gone. *Maybe he has heard me come in and is hiding?*, Kevin thought taking a few steps forward. But in the dark his foot hit some metal object on the ground which rolled around with a loud metal clang.

"Allo, il y a quelqu'un?", Pascal shouted out, wondering what had caused the noise.

Kevin realised that he could no longer hide and moved towards the young boy's voice. He was

unsure whether the boy was alone or whether he was walking into yet another trap. Kevin could feel his heart pounding with fear and anticipation.

"Hello, do you speak English?", Kevin shouted into the dark.

A torch beam cut through the dark not far from where Kevin stood, and Kevin could make out the crude bedstead the boy had built himself, with a sleeping bag, a backpack and various food wrappers strewn all around.

"A little bit …", Pascal replied in broken English. "Who are you? What do you want?"

Kevin walked towards the boy who was sitting on his sleeping bag, staring anxiously at Kevin and shining the torch into Kevin's face. Kevin could now see that the boy was alone and that he was probably about 11-years-old, slim and frail-looking, and evidently scared. Just the type of victim he needed!

"Don't worry … I am not here to harm you", Kevin lied while crouching down to be at eye level with the boy. In the faint light from the torch Kevin could see that the boy had a beautiful face, a small stubby nose, sensuous lips, dark piercing eyes, and dark black hair that looked rather dishevelled and unkempt. Judging from the food waste lying scattered around the boy, Kevin assumed that the boy must have been in this place for a while.

Staring at the boy's beautiful face and slim body gave Kevin an immediate erection. Even if he still had a day in Paris before his flight back, he could of course not wait any longer, having now found this lonely and vulnerable boy in a place where nobody could see them. He had to grab the opportunity. He knew that his sex-starved mind could not cope with another failure like Ljubljana or Moscow. He had to act now.

Kevin grabbed Pascal's arm hard and pulled the boy towards him. Although it was painful with Kevin's injury to his ribcage, the boy felt as light as a feather. He was so slim and beautiful, just the type of victim Kevin had hoped for all these past months!

"Non, non!", Pascal shouted, not understanding what was happening. "Mais qu'est-ce-que vous faites, monsieur?"

But Kevin had, yet again, become oblivious to his surroundings. His sexual urge had now completely taken over. As he had done so many times before, but almost always in less suitable locations, he expertly turned Pascal around so that he could put one arm around Pascal's neck. He quickly opened the zipper of Pascal's grimy jeans and pulled his trousers and underpants down. Pascal wiggled and struggled to get out of Kevin's grip, but he did not have the power to fight an adult man. Kevin had also unzipped his own trousers and had pulled them down, pressing his erect penis against

But just as he was about to penetrate the boy, Kevin could feel a slight pain in his head. The pain increased quickly and after a few seconds it was so intense that Kevin could no longer concentrate on what he was doing. Was this a side-effect of his earlier beating? Had the teenage boys injured his head? The pain was now so intense that Kevin had to hold his free hand against his head. It felt as if something inside his head was trying to get out, as if there was a giant lump in his head that was about to burst. The pain was now so intense that his penis went limp and a second later Kevin had to let go of the boy. He knelt next to the boy, leaned forward, and held his head with both his hands. He had never felt so much pain in his life before. His head felt as if it was about to burst.

Pascal, meanwhile, had wriggled free of Kevin's deadly embrace, had pulled up his underpants and trousers, and sat on his sleeping bag opposite Kevin, watching him intensely and with a fierce, concentrated expression on his face. Kevin was now hunched forward in so much pain that his head was almost touching the ground. *What is the boy doing to me?*, he wondered with his last shreds of lucidity. *What is happening?*

But then Kevin saw something he had never seen before. A shiny yellowish filament had begun to emanate from Pascal's forehead, winding its way towards Kevin's forehead. The searing pain

increased as the filament grew thicker, flickering in the still air of the disused factory like a breeze of air, ethereal and massless. Certain that the boy was doing this to him, and with a last desperate burst of energy, Kevin lashed out at the yellowish filament. When he touched it, it dissipated into thousands of tiny sparkles where his fingers touched it, only to reassemble again on the other side of his digits. But Kevin could not prevent the filament growing thicker. It was now a yellow radiating stream of light flickering between Pascal's and Kevin's foreheads. Suddenly, Kevin put both hands to his forehead and screamed in agony.

"Stop! Please stop!", Kevin moaned, "I am so sorry … I am sorry …"

But Pascal intensified the energy stream with his mind, and a reddish, blood-coloured substance began to be sucked out of Kevin's forehead. The blood-red filament grew in thickness and seeped out of Kevin's head at ever greater speed … and then Kevin's head exploded, showering Pascal and the immediate surroundings with thousands of fragments of Kevin's skull and brain. One of Kevin's eyeballs could be heard bobbing around the concrete floor until it came to rest near a rusty piece of discarded metal. Kevin's headless torso slumped forward and crashed onto the concrete floor. Litres of blood which gushed out of his severed carotid

artery created a large red pool at Pascal's feet and slowly soaked into Pascal's sleeping bag.

Pascal just sat there, flabbergasted at what had just happened. Everything had happened so quickly that he'd had no time to think at all. Everything he had done had been reactive. This awful man coming into his secret den, and then trying to do something to Pascal which he did not understand. But he knew that the man had strangled him hard and had hurt his anus, that the man probably would have killed him. But Pascal was also surprised at what he himself had done. He was stunned that his powers, his strange 'skill' had proved to be so deadly. Never before had he used his skill to kill another person, and he felt devastated and distraught for it. He stared down in disgust at the headless torso lying in front of him in a pool of blood. Pascal was very scared. If the police ever found out what he had done, he would certainly end up in prison for the rest of his life.

He stood up on unsteady legs. His sleeping bag was soaked in blood and now useless. Pascal knew that he could not stay here. He had to find another place. He quickly grabbed his few belongings and stuffed them into his pack, but left the blood-soaked sleeping bag lying on the floor in a tangled mass, and without glancing back at Kevin's headless body made his way to the door. He carefully peeked out and was at first blinded by the bright daylight.

Nobody could be seen on the street. Pascal quickly opened the door, slipped out, closed the door carefully and made his way down the street without looking back. He felt miserable but also relieved that he had survived what had just happened. Maybe, deep inside, he also felt a sense of pride at what he had just done. A wry smile appeared on his face. Let them try to get him! He was ready for everything now!

29

The present

Rachel gazed at the congregation that stood around the coffin that had just been lowered into the ground. The coffin contained the remains of Markus Schlesinger who could finally be laid to rest, 20 years after being raped and murdered by Kevin Miller. Thomas Schlesinger, Markus's father stood solemnly at the edge of the grave, his hands folded together. Heinz Schlesinger, Markus's uncle and Thomas's brother and DNA-donor to the ancestry site that had finally led to the successful identification of 'moorboy', stood next to Thomas, looking equally solemn. Inzuman was to the right of Rachel, Superintendent Warrington to her left, and Hazel Molfese, the Harbourtown forensic scientist, had also been able to make it to the town of Dürrkirchen in Germany where the Schlesinger family came from and where Markus's father lived.

Gazing at the small coffin being lowered into the grave, Rachel could not prevent herself from thinking how hard it had been to ring Thomas Schlesinger to tell him that his son was dead. His reply had been, as was so often the case with cases of missing children, that he had hoped for the best

but prepared for the worst, but he nonetheless broke down at the other end of the line when Rachel had confirmed that the DNA match left no doubt that the buried remains discovered on the moor were those of his son. Thomas had found it hard to believe that his son had been the first victim of a serial killer who, for 20 years, had raped and killed nearly 30 innocent boys, but he was also somewhat relieved that his son's death had at least partly led to the eventual identification of the serial killer.

Rachel, Inzuman and Warrington had been particularly relieved that Thomas Schlesinger did not blame them for failing to solve the mystery of the disappearance of his son 20 years ago. After Inzuman had explained to him how difficult it can be to identify bodies and to match them up with the surprisingly long list of missing boys anywhere in the world, Thomas had confirmed that this case had probably also been made more complicated by the fact that he and his son had only intended to stay in Harbourtown briefly and that, after Thomas' brief secondment at the Harbourtown military base as a technical consultant for the nuclear submarines based at Harbourtown, he had returned to Germany soon after Markus had disappeared. Thomas had confided in Rachel and Inzuman that Markus had had a very hard time at Harbourtown College, partly because he was a German kid in what was a relatively parochial and bigoted part of the UK, but

also because his mum had died just earlier which had left Markus in a fragile psychological state. Thomas admitted that, because of this, the possibility that Markus had just run away had always been at the back of his mind. And the fact that he had then returned to Germany soon after Markus's disappearance had also complicated the search for his missing son. But then, he also admitted, he had always hoped that, one day, his son would re-appear and turn up at the doorstep of their family home in Dürrkirchen. At least now he had certainty about what had happened, even with the dreadful knowledge that his son's death must have been very gruesome.

Rachel found all this very sad. In the end, there could be no winners here but only losers. Serial killers always left a trail of utter devastation behind them, and finally solving the case could not bring any real closure to the bereaved families. She found it hard to supress her tears at the tragic fate of moorboy, and she saw that both Inzuman and Hazel also struggled to keep their emotions at bay.

But Rachel's thoughts also quickly turned to the weird and tragic end of Kevin Miller himself. They had quickly found out from Kevin's secretary and colleagues that he had gone to a resilience conference in Paris, and Rachel, Stefan and Inzuman had immediately flown to Paris and caught up with their Parisian colleagues who were just

getting details of a strange death inside a derelict factory in the poor district of Branlieu. Initially, Rachel, Stefan and Inzuman had not dared think that there could be a link between this strange incident and their serial killer, but the fact that the dead person was indeed Kevin Miller had quickly been established when the Parisian police compared the dead body's DNA with that of Kevin Miller.

Rachel and her colleagues had quickly been brought into the investigation by their French colleagues, but nobody understood what had happened. It was evident that Kevin's head had exploded from inside, and that there was no evidence of outside interference such as a blow to the head or a bullet wound. Nobody in either the French or British police force had ever seen anything like it, and nobody could explain what had happened. The fact that Kevin's headless torso was part-naked suggested that maybe this was another attempt at a rape of a boy, but the only item found with the body was a blood-soaked sleeping bag, and there was no evidence that Kevin had assaulted a boy in this unlikely place. The police thought that the sleeping bag probably belonged to homeless people who occasionally used the abandoned factory building for shelter. The case remained open, but the Paris colleagues were uncertain as to whether this case would ever be fully solved.

In many ways this was a very unsatisfactory ending for Rachel and her colleagues. They knew that they had been very close on the heels of the killer, and she was sure that they would have apprehended Kevin Miller in Paris eventually. But she was less certain whether they could have prevented another boy rape and murder before they caught him. So maybe the strange accident that befell Kevin did prevent his final murder? They probably would never know, but at least no further boy murders had been reported in Paris around that time, so they knew that Kevin Miller's deadly killing spree across Europe had finally come to an end.

Rachel looked up from the grave. German burial ceremonies were different from those in the UK, and she was unsure what would come next. The brief speeches were over and the congregation began to dissipate. Thomas Schlesinger still stood by the side of his son's grave. He looked up and briefly nodded towards Rachel and her colleagues. Deep sorrow was evident in his wry smile. Rachel smiled back, but she felt very uncomfortable about the whole situation. Had they done as much as they could to solve this immensely sad case? She knew that the moorboy case would stay with her for the rest of her life.

Very slowly, Inzuman, Warrington, Hazel and Rachel made their way back to their rental car,

parked near the cemetery gates. It would be a long and solemn drive back to the airport.

Printed in Dunstable, United Kingdom